Up, Do

Flash Fiction by
Women Writers

Edited by

Patricia Flaherty Pagan

Up, Do: Flash Fiction by Women Writers
© 2014 by Patricia Flaherty Pagan

ISBN: 978-0-9914176-0-5

Library of Congress Control Number: 2014900827

Cover art: "Hope Is a Thing With Wings"
by Jodi Sh. Doff

Spider Road Press
Houston, Texas
www.spiderroadpress.com

Dedicated to the teachers, in and out of the classroom, who showed me that girls' musings and women's words are key ingredients in the alchemy of storytelling.

Contents

IV Our Dreams; Our Nightmares   71

Up, Do

Flash Fiction by
Women Writers

Introduction

I subscribe to the theory that flash fiction is like a geode of a larger narrative. Slicing through the characters and the highest arc of the plot, the flash writer reveals the crystals shining within. Every movement of the blade, every word typed on the page, is crucial. It is a form I myself feel drawn to explore.

I started bouncing around the idea of a flash fiction collection by self-defined women writers when I read the distressing 2012 VIDA Count report. Even in the supposedly progressive days of 2012, American literary journals were publishing more book reviews and short stories written by men than by women. Yet my female writer friends were bravely sending out their short stories, reviews and novels night after night. Didn't their writing deserve a home? It did indeed. My love of flash fiction and my desire to promote the equal treatment of women's words worked in concert to lead me to curate this anthology.

"Up, Do" is a two-way command. I believe that women's ideas and actions can propel us all — male, female, transgendered — upward. The next great flash fiction writer is out there writing, revising and honing her craft. Her ideas will inform us all. Go ahead. Find her. Go ahead. Be her.

Patricia Flaherty Pagan

I

Our Hearts

"Bleeding Heart"
by Jesi Bender

To the Israeli Who Danced with Me on My Twenty-First Birthday

Jessica Lynne Henkle

You don't know that I measure my cereal, or that I eat the same six mini-meals every day because I've already done the math on the calories they contain. You don't know I'm addicted to running, that I can break a sweat in the frigid Boston winter, logging miles upon miles alone along the Charles. Blessed stranger, when you spot me hovering near the bar of the Liquor Store — the crowded club I've been dragged to against my will — you don't know the Cosmopolitan I'm clutching, vodka and sugar growing tepid in the thin plastic cup, is the first hard liquor I've ever tasted.

You don't know of my years spent declining drinks at parties — my years spent declining parties — or that the bejeweled blouse I'm wearing belongs to my roommate. You don't know I don't own any clothing that sparkles, or that these shiny black stilettos that bring us eye-to-eye were purchased for a costume. Praise you for seeing only my blonde hair, the rhinestone stud in my nose, my slim physique, which I pretend you assume is thanks to good genes, and not the aforementioned hours spent straining as the breath pulls from my lungs into clouds that come faster the longer I run. Praise you for not knowing I'll finish college in three years.

When you approach, you say nothing, just take my hand and start dancing, and I am too polite to say *stop*. I press one palm to yours, the other to the neck of your brown leather jacket, and let you spin me in the swirl of bodies and air thickened with heat. Let our whirling spill the remnants of my half-drunk cocktail on the already sticky floor, let you speak into my ear — lips moist on my skin — the way no lover ever has, and praise you for not knowing I've only had one. All night, I don't dance with other men, and when the club closes at two, you don't know I'll be the one ensuring my wasted friends get home safely.

While the crowd breaks up around us, you hold me. You ask for my number, and when I summon that temporarily forgotten courage to say *no*, you smile and pull back, but take my hand and kiss it, before you walk away. I don't move. I watch you go. We don't know I'll still think of you years later, never accepting that I cannot remember your name, a part of me still wishing I'd been a girl who says *yes*.

Paris 1976

Janet Garber

"Just give me 10 minutes," he said. Several minutes later, he emerged from the bathroom, stopping in the kitchen to add salt to the soup and to mention that the floor was rather sticky.

Our small refrigerator, affectionately dubbed, "le frigo," did not even have a freezer compartment, which necessitated a lot of shopping every day. I was lucky not to be putting our milk and cheese out the kitchen window ledge.

We sat down at the small foldout table by the window to our typical French summertime meal of fresh vegetable soup, salad from his mother's garden, cheese from La Laiterie, bread from the Engels' bakery, and fruit from the Arab market.

When we were both working, if he got home first and prepared dinner, he used to joke, "Look, I cooked you a salad." Now that I was home with the baby, there were no jokes.

"Let's stop this, Pierre. Don't you see the baby is yelling so his voice is louder than ours? He can tell we're arguing."

"Yes, ok, but I'm tired of your *soupe a la grimace*. Be happy, dammit!"

I frowned. Why must my unhappiness be my fault — why wouldn't he take his share of blame?

"Pierre, let's go out tomorrow night. Madeleine Renaud is at the Theatre d'Orsay during Beckett's *O les beaux jours*. You know how I'm dying to see that."

"Yes, maybe." He frowned into his soup.

"We could eat in the Marais, hop the metro or the No. 69 bus, and have a nice evening."

"Wait a minute, Luce. If you go to the theatre, you don't need to eat out too."

"But I don't want to be bothered cooking before we go out," I whined.

"Lucie!" We both looked at the baby, whose chirping had gotten rather high-pitched in the last few minutes. He was like a barometer for our fights. Are we really fighting or just discussing? Let's ask the baby.

Pierre picked the baby out of his seat and went off to the bedroom to play with him. I was stuck doing the dishes and cleanup. In the old days, before baby, at least once in a while, with a great show of altruism, Pierre would don a little white apron his mother had sewn together out of two Lin des Vosges dishtowels, pull closed the kitchen curtain and set to work. First he would fill the basin with hot water. Then he would add an infinitesimal drop of detergent. For quite a while he would appear to be busy, soaking and scrubbing the dishes, glasses, utensils, and frying pan. At some point he would decide it was all clean enough, drain the basin of soapy water, and in a thin trickle of clean cold water, rinse the dishes and set them in the drainer to dry. It was quite a ritual, and it took some time. He would beam with pride afterwards and assure me that not many French husbands would be caught dead doing such a thing.

And oh the time he was caught! Mme. Jean, our Polish neighbor of 75 or so, who was practically family and took liberties as such, happened to sneak up on us in the kitchen one night after dinner. There was Pierre at the sink. They both let out a shriek. It couldn't have been more scandalous had she walked in on us fornicating. In fact, both would have been considerably less embarrassed at that, Europeans being what they are.

Chuckling at the memory of Mme. Jean solemnly pledging not to repeat what she had seen, I didn't notice Pierre had come back into the kitchen. He reached over and shut off the Niagara-like flow of steaming hot water I used to wash the dishes.

"Oh Mama, I think this little fellow wants to be changed."

"Can't Papa take care of him then?"

"Remember, Luce, I told you this morning I had to go back to the lab tonight to finish work on a project I'm doing with Claude."

"How nice."

"I wish, Luce, you would be more supportive of my work."

I spent the evening, my only time for adult companionship, curled up on the studio bed (our "couch") in the living room, reading, writing letters.

Later that night, at 3 a.m., baby screeched awake. Pierre scolded, "You can't keep getting up like this. You're spoiling him. You're wearing yourself out."

I was already up and running. There seemed to be noise on all sides of me, ricocheting off the walls, but it was only Pierre in one ear, baby in the other. I plugged in the bottle warmer, fetched a bottle from le frigo, then scooped up one ugly, red, almost evil-looking little monster from his crib. He looked so like his daddy.

"Kiddo," I said, "It's a good thing you're good looking or you would've been in the trash by now."

And I tried hard to hug away his anger.

We Decided

Kathryn Kulpa

We decided he would have dark hair, long and wavy and unruly, because he was someone who could not be ruled. He would have dark eyes, dark as bittersweet chocolate melted on the stove. He would be pale and wan. He would be haunted and melancholy.

We didn't know the word Byronic yet but if we had he would have been that, in a heartbeat. One of us did know Mr. Rochester. One of us knew Wolverine, and Tony Stark.

We had questions for which our parents had no answers. Perhaps there were no answers. We didn't talk to God. We talked to Judy Blume.

We both drew pictures. We both wrote stories. In our secret hearts we knew that one of us wrote better stories than the other, one of us drew better pictures. It didn't matter. We could be a collective genius, like Gilbert & Sullivan, like Lennon & McCartney. We would always be together.

We decided he had fantastic and dangerous talents. We decided he was an international spy. A thrilling daredevil. A genius, blessed and cursed with a lapidary brilliance as far beyond the minds of ordinary humans as ordinary humans were beyond the minds of banana slugs.

We decided he had a fortress of solitude. A bat cave. A secret place only he could know.

We grew our breasts. We got our periods.

We decided he had a girlfriend. Only to her would he appear as himself, throwing off all disguises. And she would lay his tired head in her lap and sing him to sleep, singing a song so old no one alive could remember when it was new.

Then we decided she was boring, and we killed her.

We decided we liked her better dead. And now he had a secret sorrow, a scar on his heart that no merely beautiful woman could heal.

We decided he had vices. A past he didn't talk about. A black car he drove too fast. And when some girl called out to him, "Be careful," as some girl inevitably did, he only laughed. A sardonic, reckless laugh.

We learned to kiss. We learned to lie.

We decided he was an international playboy. We decided he had 1,000 girls a week. One of us who was mathematically inclined decided this worked out to a new girl for every six minutes.

We decided this figure was possible.

Later, we decided that boys who kissed us behind open locker doors in school corridors and on the roofs of our parents' cars at drive-ins were less expert lovers. But some of them, we discovered, were just as adroit at stringing along multiple girls.

We decided deception was hardly heroic.

We decided all those girls were a distraction. Somewhere, deep inside himself, he needed to be saved. He needed a woman. *The* woman. One who could see through his brilliant, brutal shell and heal the wounded boy inside.

And she would be dark and small and soft-eyed and quiet.

Or she would be fair and tall and brazen-eyed and laughing.

We decided we could not decide. Democracy has its limits. In some contests only a bloody coup will do. Only a mangled body, lying dead in the wreck of a black car.

We learned to drive. We learned to leave.

We decided we had outgrown each other. Decided sharply and without mercy, the way girls do.

Years later we met at parties. We left lipsticked smiles in wine glasses and exchanged false compliments on each other's dresses.

Politely, the way murderers do.

The Dance

Catherine Edmunds

Mehmet's figures dance across the canvas, hold hands, pull each other into mist-colors and flashes of light from the sunset at the far end of the street. Janine wants this fire dance, these spike-legged figures. She wants their movement, their life. She sees a face in one of them and pretends it's her. Because he'd paint her, wouldn't he?

She turns to the Neolithic pot in the glass display cabinet. Following its black scratches, she remembers making something similar at school. Her dad was an archaeologist and she wanted him to see her but it was Mum who put flowers in the pot. The water leaked out, so purple asters from the garden were replaced with dried grasses, but they gathered dust. Still Dad never noticed, even though he'd grown the grasses. He'd be out in his shed hewing a chopping board out of the wood of an old apple tree with blunt iron instruments, his thoughts back at Watendlath, far, far away, striking the back of a chisel with a mallet that used to hit the windbreak into the ground on chilled Northumbrian beaches, but he's not even there — he's crossing the old packhorse bridge with a flock of Herdwick sheep.

Janine closes her eyes. She imagines the sheep smell, the lanolin, the roughness of a fleece, droppings, tufted grass, sticky and dangerous sundews.

Mehmet paints his parents, his childhood; children dancing down the alley way beneath the tall arches that stop the buildings from falling into each other. The cobbles run with stench, the windows don't line up and the walls are black with slime at the base, but the smell is his childhood, his sisters and their dolls, always dancing.

Janine only knows lakes and he's of the desert; his mother, black-robed, sewing. Her mother, beige-slacked, smoking, telling her dad, 'That pipe stinks.' Sending him out to the shed, together with his pipe rack, his tins, his cleaners, his hurt; while she smokes her half-size ciggies because 'they're better for you.' No dancing allowed. Too much fun is bad for you. A little ballet perhaps, but no tap.

Mehmet's sisters dance through their childhood and into marriage; dance their babies on their laps. Mehmet can't see Janine because she can't dance, so she joins a class, laughs at herself, still can't dance. Fuckit! Can't dance. Leaves. Marries an uptight solicitor from Tosser, Screwit, Fuckup and Soddem, or whatever they were called. She's past caring.

She once loved a man called Mehmet. He never painted her.

She keeps a clay pot on the mantelpiece, made at school more than sixty years ago. It's stuffed with treasures: her children's baby teeth; a newspaper clipping of an art exhibition a long time ago; dried grasses; dust; pipe cleaners; a twist of Old Virginia Flake; dried-up apple pips.

From her cottage window she watches the Herdwick sheep dance across the old packhorse bridge.

The Understudy

Miranda Stone

Kayla and I sat at the kitchen table eating peanut butter sandwiches while our mother writhed on the floor.

"I've sacrificed everything for you girls," Mama wailed, beating her fists against her chest. Her nightgown rode up her thighs. "I have nothing left to give."

Kayla put down her sandwich and clapped. "Bravo, Mama," she said. "You've dazzled us with yet another stellar performance. Now get off the damn floor."

Mama cried harder, and then she began to retch, her face the color of an unripe plum. I rolled my eyes, and Kayla just shook her head. "I've had enough of this, Mama," she said, raising her voice to be heard over the racket. "Eighteen years I've lived in this house and watched you destroy our lives. You ran Daddy off—"

"Don't talk about that man!" Mama yanked hard at the roots of her dark hair.

"I don't blame him a bit for leaving," Kayla went on. "I can't believe he stayed as long as he did. We're all sick of your promises to get sober."

"I will," Mama said, struggling to sit up. She turned to me, her eyes wide and pleading. "You believe me, don't you, Sylvia? You know your mama loves you."

Before I could answer, Kayla leaned forward so she was at Mama's eye level. "Why would she believe you?" she said through her teeth. "Just last week you stole her babysitting money so you could buy another fifth of vodka." Kayla's pale blue eyes darkened to gray. "You're a worthless drunk."

Mama covered her ears and screamed. I felt my pulse in the center of my forehead, a dull nauseating throb. "Mama, be quiet," I shouted. "The neighbors will call the cops again."

Kayla leapt from her chair and grabbed Mama's wrists. "You listen to me," she said, her jaw muscles twitching. Mama struggled and snarled like a wild animal, but Kayla was stronger. She pulled Mama's hands from her ears. "I'm leaving this goddamn house tomorrow. You hear me? I'm leaving. Just like Daddy."

My face grew hot, the way it always did before I threw up. I began to shake, my knees knocking together under the table.

Mama fell silent. She searched Kayla's face as my sister's words registered.

"Kayla, no," I choked. The tears I swallowed gathered in my throat.

Kayla glanced at me, and her eyes softened. Mama took advantage of her distraction and raked her nails over the tender skin of Kayla's throat. Kayla delivered a hard slap to our mother's cheek. Then she tossed Mama away from her and stood.

"No," Mama said, lunging at my sister. She wrapped her arms around Kayla's legs. "You can't leave me. Honey, you don't mean it."

Kayla scrunched her eyes shut. "Mama, let me go, or I'll beat the shit out of you."

I scrambled over to Mama and grabbed her shoulders. "You're drunk," I said, struggling to loosen her grip on Kayla. "You need to sleep it off."

"Kayla, I love you," Mama sobbed. "Don't go."

Kayla didn't look at either of us as she fled the kitchen. Mama reached for me and pulled my head to her chest. "You have to make her stay, Sylvia."

I squirmed in her embrace. "I'll talk to Kayla," I said. "Just go to bed, okay?" With effort I pried her off me and left her sitting on the kitchen floor.

My sister's door was shut tight. I knocked softly. "Kayla, open up."

She pulled the door open and peered over my shoulder. "Where is she?"

"In the kitchen." I stepped into Kayla's tiny bedroom.

"Don't try to change my mind," Kayla said as she shut the door and locked it.

I whirled to face her. "You can't leave me here," I said.

Kayla looked down at the worn carpet, circling a dark stain with the toe of her shoe. "I'm sorry, Sylvia. But I always told you I'd get out of here as soon as I could. Now that I've saved up enough money from waiting tables, I can move into my own place."

"Take me with you," I said, holding out my hands. "I'll work and help pay the rent. I'll cook and clean so you won't have to lift a finger."

Kayla shook her head sadly. "You're just sixteen. You have to stay here."

I slumped onto her bed. "I'll lose my mind," I said. My voice sounded distant to my own ears. "I'll end up a wreck just like Mama."

Kayla wrapped her arms around me. I rested my aching head against the pilled fabric of her sweater. "No, you won't," she whispered. We stayed that way for a long time, and I would have let her hold me forever, but she finally said, "Sylvia, I've got to finish packing."

I went to sit in the dark living room, relieved that Mama had gone to bed. Perched in the wooden rocker by the front window, I waited for the grandfather clock to chime twice. Then I made my way to the kitchen, where I fumbled through the drawer next to the stove until my fingers closed on the handle of a suitable knife.

Outside, the frigid December air stung my face. Kayla's old Toyota sat in the driveway, and I strode toward it without hesitation. Squatting next to the right front tire, I drove the knife blade in deep and heard the satisfying hiss of escaping air. I made a circle around the car, flattening each tire as I went and then stepped back as the car inched toward the pavement.

Closing my eyes, I stood in the glow of the streetlight and imagined the scene that would unfold in the morning. Kayla would scream and swear. She'd strike me and say she hated me, and I'd fall to my knees before her, weeping as I begged for forgiveness. And Mama would beam while I acted out her old role, knowing she couldn't have performed it better.

Facing Window

Janette Ayachi

Across the street in the facing window, I watch the same woman every night. She leaves the curtains open to dream under the sky. It verifies her existence, helps her to breathe. Most nights she gets drunk and plays guitar. She pauses a lot and always needs the music out in front of her. She has a terrible memory. She stops when her fingers hurt or when the kids start to distract her or when the wine dries out. I have been a proud voyeur watching her for years. If she moves out I will be lost. Sometimes I want to leave her gifts in the stairwell. Somehow I think that we are connected, lined up in our tenement buildings like figurines, by a higher power. Somehow I think that we are aligned like the stars.

She has not been sleeping recently. I watch her yawn under the blue light of her computer screen, tapping the keys and tugging at her hair. I know that this is love. I have seen her naked, bending in the half-light like a Degas ballerina sculpted in bronze, sworn into position for eternity behind glass. Her body has carried children. She avoids mirrors. She stands against walls, and her hourglass silhouette shatters into bats in the moonlight. I drink to understand her and then worry about her in the mornings as she stares down to the empty streets, the coffee's steam evaporating the glass.

Yesterday she danced, broke arabesque shapes into clumsy freestyle, wore oversized sunglasses in the bedroom and sipped wine in shots. The kids jumped on the bed, and she led pirouettes, swinging them around like puppets. They all laughed a lot, until one of the kids fell from the bed and the light switched off.

She is always tidying up during the day, and I'm sure she curses as she stutters through the tasks. When the sun shines in through the window I see the sharp creases across her face. I hide behind my plant at the window, peering through the openings of leaves like an explorer spying on a rare and dangerous habitat, focused on going unnoticed. She has never seen me, only her own reflection in the glass, the trees glowing under the streetlamp and the rugged curve of Arthur's Seat in the background. But it is always the sky that strikes her attention, the various shades of blue, the faces in the clouds, and the aluminum constellations.

She is learning to trust the universe and then to trust herself. I avoid her in the streets. I am obsessed now, tuned in and turned on. I eat my meals at the window, sleep near the window, watch and wait, adapt to the fuzzy channels, climb heights to fix the aerial. I pace the floors and enjoy the sound of my own footsteps; tell-tale-hearts are trapped in my walls — I balance out her nocturnal rhythms. I keep all the lights dim and rarely leave the apartment.

I have been depressed for a long time now, but the woman in the facing window encourages me to focus, keeps me functioning, and helps me to breath. She is my sky, her various shades of blue, her faces in the clouds, and her constellation of activity star-marked around each room.

One evening, I opened the blinds and my heart emptied itself on the floor like a burst drain. There was a woman spying on me from the facing window, dipping her head behind a plant — the kids pulled at my sleeves to drag me to dance.

Seven Years

Theo Greenblatt

If you had been alone for seven years, you might allow your-self to fall in love. It could start with glances and smiles, and talk about children and poets and pets.

You might admire his attachment to his family. After the first innocuous email, you would begin to look for his responses. First, twice a day, then three times, then four times daily. Your exchanges would be witty and esoteric, and the double entendre would be mild, equivocal, even.

He would say to you one day, over coffee in a pizza parlor reeking of garlic and disinfectant, that when you pushed up the sleeve of your sweater the sight of your forearm made him hard. So you might agree to kiss him in the parking lot.

It's possible you would have him completely alone just once, on a sunny January morning when your children were at school — your first conjugation in seven years. He might bring a split of champagne, maybe a BB King CD, and a six-pack of condoms, like a box of promises. You would be so anxious that you couldn't actu-ally feel the excitement until it became a memory. He would never go this far again, but afterwards you would press him to kiss you in an elevator or the shadowed stairwell of a building. You might even go down on him in his steamed-up car parked by the ocean when you both swore you were only going to have lunch together.

You might cry and throw your favorite casserole dish across the room if, one windy night, your internet connection went down and you couldn't check your email.

The memory of his touch, played over and over, would always be more potent than the experience itself. If you had been alone for seven years, and even before that no man had understood your language, you could go on with this man for a long time. You would not quite starve because he would keep feeding you with words. You might find yourself willing to live that way indefinitely, surviving on a diet of poetry and euphemism.

Then one day you might overhear him feeding words to someone else. They would be familiar words, words that you had sucked on for their sweetness late at night, sitting alone at your computer screen. Or they might be words that you had fed to him, and he regurgitated, like a bird feeding its young. Your words would be the richest ones because you would have been saving them for so long before you lavished them on this man. This married man.

If you had been alone for seven years, you could fall in love with a married man, but it would probably end this way. And even if you knew that right from the start, you still would not say no to that first garlic kiss in the parking lot.

Colorado

J. Christine Johnson

Jess steered her tottering Datsun around the potholes, parking outside the fence so the engine wouldn't wake the sleepers in the tipi. Her wrists ached from the heavy plates heaped with enchiladas and refried beans, her feet throbbed from the concrete floor, she reeked of lard and sweat. When she closed her eyes, she saw tickets scribbled with "B GR, X SALSA, NO SC" and heard the cook, Russ, shouting, "'B space GR is for Burrito Grande. B-G-R is for Burger. Can you handle that?"

Patsy was waiting for her in the shed Darcy had converted into a kitchen. She sat in the recliner, pushing her toe against the floor to gently rock the chair. The cats, which used the sides and the back of the recliner as a scratching post, had raked its plaid upholstery to shreds.

Jess could see Patsy's breath in the small circle of hollow light cast by a kerosene lantern. Darcy wouldn't allow Patsy and Jess to feed the woodstove after sunset. They were meant to bed down in the tipi when the light failed. No one took into account that Jess's shifts ended after midnight, when the last table was reset for breakfast and the floors were mopped to the door.

Jess had met Patsy and Darcy at a canning class in Delta in September. When she came to class one Saturday with a split lip, they offered her shelter in their large tipi outside of Cedaredge. Free of charge, just help with groceries and cooking.

When she confessed a couple of weeks ago that she was two months pregnant, they told her they would like to adopt the baby. When Jess laughed, she saw Darcy's hazel eyes fade to dull mud.

Jess set her purse and car keys on the wooden cable spindle that had been turned on one end to make a round table. "Patsy, you all right? Why are you up so late?" As Jess approached, she could see a small book in Patsy's lap.

Patsy picked up the book and held it to the light. Jess recognized the fabric cover printed with purple and maroon flowers. It was her journal.

"Darcy was cleaning the tipi," Patsy said in a flat voice. "This fell off your cot and opened up. We saw our names, so we read what you wrote about us. I know it wasn't right what we did. But you shouldn't have written about us. We'd like you to leave in the morning."

Patsy rose and walked toward her with the journal. Jess extended her hand. Patsy set the book in her palm and it opened like a hymnal. Patsy slid open the glass door and walked away, leaving the door open behind her. The cold air felt solid. It braced Jess upright when it seemed her knees would give way.

She stood trembling for a few minutes, thinking of the box beneath her bed where she had hid her journal that morning, as she did every morning.

Outside, her Datsun still ticked as it cooled in the November air. Mist had settled into Surface Creek Valley and it smelled of frost and wood smoke. Jess imagined the mist slipping down the slopes of Grand Mesa, hiding Cedaredge from the moon that tipped light onto the San Juan Mountains.

Jess turned her key in the ignition. A deer bolted in front of the car and leapt to the scrub oak beyond. She felt as frightened as the deer. And as free. The car rolled down the gravel driveway.

Supermom

Donna Hill

It was my daughter's seventeenth birthday. August. Hot as hell that day. My son and grandson were much younger, running around the house playing while I was busy preparing for my daughter's party. I cooked and cleaned and monitored the boys, all the while making mental lists of all the things I still needed to do before the party started. Before my baby came home to her party.

And I wasn't thinking, not paying attention, trying to do too many things at once — because I could — so I lifted the chicken from the pan of boiling hot grease with the fork. I didn't hold the pan like I should have and somehow, as frying chicken will do, it stuck, and I pulled and lifted the pan and the chicken and the grease all at once, down my legs and onto the linoleum floor.

The heat of the grease was so hot that it was cold when it slapped against my skin. It must have been cold because I froze as if time stopped and then the searing heat seeped past the protection of my skin and woke up the nerves, and I screamed from the pain that had become human, taking on life atop flesh that was turning unrecognizable.

I screamed even as the skin began to bubble and the linoleum warp. I screamed from the unimaginable pain that shook my body.

I screamed, knowing that now I would not have my baby's birthday party ready in time.

A Matter of Time

Tania Moore

I was putting away the groceries when Liam called to tell me that he had accidentally gotten on an express train, and could I pick him up in town, one stop away?

Liam and I did not have the kind of marriage where we depended on each other for rides to and from the train, but I was not annoyed by his call, perhaps because both children were away, Clarissa at a summer internship in Palo Alto, Gideon working as a camp counselor in Maine. For perhaps the first time in twenty-two years, no one would notice if dinner was late.

"I'll be there in five minutes," I said.

As I drove down the driveway, air rushed through the open windows, and for an instant I forgot that my hands were on the wheel, solid, weighted with bone, even as something cleaved free — wrenched asunder by the wind. Time slipped a groove, and I was no longer fifty, but twenty-five, meeting Liam for drinks after work in the city. There were no children, only summer, pouring in eddies over my toenails, painted then, as now, lapis lazuli blue. I steered down Half Moon Lane, passing the creek where Gideon and Clarissa would throw leaves and sticks while I listened to the whispering susurration of water churning downstream, but this was not the Volkswagen Rabbit with the rusted undercarriage that Liam and I drove across Europe. This car was covered in white enamel, with leather seats, while across the tracks a slumbering river, pregnant with the weight of living currents, refracted the setting sun.

I waited at the light while commuters disgorged from the train. Those who were not swallowed by waiting mini-vans or

Lexuses spilled across the street, straining against gravity as they ascended Main Street's steep hill. My body, too, remembered this human flow, streaming out from subway tunnels, released to scatter wherever heart or humor led. There were no houses or cars or children, only a vivid past and limitless future.

The light changed, and I scanned the station platform, searching for Liam in the thinning crowd. I did not see him — this man who ate and slept and occasionally burped on our journey downstream over rocks like burls on a tree, catching the wails of our children as they tossed beauty and turmoil into our laps — but then he appeared by the side of the road. He raised his hand, but where was Liam's thick, curly hair? When had he started wearing a suit?

How could he be both Liam and not Liam, just as I was I, only not I, at the same time? When ice cubes clinked in our glasses, and we flagged a cab that catapulted down the avenue, light after flickering light, tearing passion and indomitable hope from our lungs.

II

Our Bodies

"Chelle" by Jesi Bender

Nothing is Wrong With Carrie

Carmen Rinehart

The exercise seemed simple enough. I hoped to lift my self-esteem by marking positive aspects of my body with a washable marker. Anything I liked about my naked body got a green mark, giving me a multisensory reinforcement. So I could see it on my skin. Feel it on my skin. Believe it in my head.

Unfortunately, I decided that with the good must come the bad. So I marked anything I didn't like with red.

The mess I made of myself breaks down like this. My big blue eyes were circled green. I always liked them. Along with my full pink lips, and my precision-shaped eyebrows. The nails on my hands were scribbled green as well as my ankles and feet. Through thick and thin, my skinny feet and ankles were always a source of pride. I wore sandals and clam diggers all year long, convinced they made me look ten pounds thinner.

Now the rest of me looked like a bloody mess. I had crossed out the shingle scars on my stomach. Imagine a sixth grader so stressed out over losing enough weight for middle school dance team try-outs that she breaks out into shingles! I didn't even make the first cut, and I have the scars to remind me. My double chin, butt, thighs, as well as the saggy tire that hangs from my hips, were scribbled on fiercely as if the marker contained a magic elixir that would melt away the unwanted cellulite and lift the skin. I couldn't reach the areas on my back or arms very well but decided that I didn't need a "multisensory" experience to remember I hate them as well.

Lastly, my breasts looked like they were decorated for Christmas. I liked the size, but not the shape. So, I got creative and drew little ornaments of each color all over them. Kind of weird I guess, but I considered it a "sensory enhancement." On second thought, now I might never look at a Christmas tree the same way ever again.

"This might not have been a great idea," I whisper to a ceiling that is beginning to shade itself in hues of scarlet. There are more negatives than positives, and my self-esteem is plummeting. I need to do something fast, or I might resort to ordering a tub of pork-fried rice from the mediocre Chinese restaurant down the street.

"What sort of self-help is this?" questions the painted girl I see in the mirror. She starts to cry.

Tears begin to wash the red from my chin and little angry drops roll down my neck. I realize that I have to take action. Wallowing in pity will just allow my self-loathing to collect on my perfect skinny feet. They are supposed to be green!

"Dry your tears and pull it together," the young woman in the mirror demands.

Grabbing a blue marker, I am determined to write positive words on all of the areas that I colored red. A purple "Brilliant" appears on one cheek, "Courageous" on the other. My stomach soon has "Forgiveness" scripted across it. Thigh number one becomes "Strong" while thigh number two becomes "Fearless." My hips are "Funny" and "Friendly." Finally, three simple words grace my backside, and I must remember to repeat them as often as possible: "You are beautiful."

Beginning

Mick Harris

I'm sitting in the basement on the lap of a Portuguese guy with psoriasis who looks like a bulldog with his finger pointing play-gun style in the small of my back.

Does this bother you?

I look down at my boots. No.

Then you'll be fine. That's the worst thing that you're ever gonna have happen to you. You suck dick?

I scoot to the edge of his knee, enough so I can turn around. No!

What would you say if someone were to ask you?

I'd say I don't do that kind of thing.

I sit down on the rusty floor safe, facing him and the girl who's sitting next to him. She's petite and gorgeous in a neon orange net dress and, aside from giving my t-shirt, miniskirt and suede boots a pitying once-over, has ignored me completely. She holds herself still with the utter attention to detail meant to freeze me out, let me know I don't belong here.

The girl laughs, and so does he. Wrong. You say it's against the law.

The safe leeches cold into my skin, but my cheeks heat up, silly little girl. You said the wrong thing, idiot.

Frankie looks at me over the tops of his plastic-rimmed Polo glasses.

You start Friday. If you still want to waitress, the job's open, but you'll make more money dancing. Be here by 11.

Violet takes me to Adam and Eve to buy my first outfit and shoes. The store is staffed by sex-positive workers, all women, whose friendliness and curiosity make me want to hide back in the car, give Violet cash and tell her to pick something for me. Still, I'm excited. I pick out a blue lace panel dress that smoothes every bump and curve into one long line of come-hither sexiness. The lace tickles my skin but it's so sheer I feel like I'm wearing nothing at all but for its structure, molding my body into stripper form. If I suck in my stomach just a little, I look like I'm a size 2, cock my hips to the side, and I'm a Robert Palmer video vixen.

My new shoes are standard black, six inches. Training heels. I wobble around the house in them for a few days in PJs, jeans, underwear, and a t-shirt. Strutting when no one's home, trying to make my steps confident without my ankles rolling. The straps cut across my toes and the plush pillowed lining doesn't do much to cushion the ball of my foot, where all my weight sits.

It takes an hour of careful shaving to remove every patch of hair on my body. Legs and armpits I'm used to, but it takes nearly a full can of floral-scented cream to make any headway on my coarse pubic hair. Violet hands me a razor and the can with solemnity, and we crack up. She sings Neil Diamond through the door.

Girl, we croon, yowling the guitar notes, *you'll be a woman, soon!*

I've never done more than trim my pubes before, not even in the summer when going to the beach means seeing the dark hair curling out of the same bikini I've had since my first year of college and pressing my legs together, willing the boys who walk by not to look at me, look at your tan girlfriends, not me.

I don't know that it's easier to cut the hair short before shaving so I glop on the cream, swirling little peaks of hair into the foam, and run the Bic over my skin repeatedly until the long curls thin out. Bending over on my knees with the showerhead pouring water over my back, it's still impossible to really guide the razor into my ass, but I manage not to nick the delicate skin there, a small miracle. This is shearing, exposing, giving up a secret. I focus on the air and water touching my skin, the hard plastic in a place nothing has ever been, and try not to think of this as some sort of loss, of moving back to girlhood.

My first day I don't eat breakfast. I take the bus downtown with my new outfit in a bright plastic yellow bag, and I have to wait outside for twenty minutes in the sun because I'm early.

A woman with teased blonde hair opens the door. Her name is Lily. She's the wife of the owner, she's really happy to meet me, and she's sure I'm going to like it here. Downstairs Frankie takes over. This is where you get dressed, he gestures, there are counters on both sides, just pick a spot. Any locker that's open is fine, did you bring a lock? My lock is left over from middle school, blue dial covered in purple sparkle nail polish, the combo written on the back in ancient sharpie.

I have an Almay blue eye accent kit from Walgreens with a color-by-numbers chart on the back — this is where the brown goes, this blue accents your brow. It's the only makeup I have, but it makes my eyes look really blue, or maybe it's the dress that does that. I don't have any idea how to do my hair so I smear some gel through the shaggier part of my chin-length bob. It's growing out into a boy's bowl cut. Frankie comes over from the office and nods at me. You look good, might need to work on it. How do you feel?

I shake my head. Really nervous. I'm shaking again, I'm afraid my bladder's about to let go. Frankie puts his hands on my shoulders and guides me over to the mirror. His breath smells like old smoke.

Look at yourself.

Lean, sexy, and smooth but awkward baby bird with legs that don't work yet, shoulders sloped to hide how exposed my breasts feel. Sweat collects between my legs.

You look good, he repeats. You're gonna be fine.

Fancy Ladies

Melanie Griffin

The boy tottered to a stop in front of the plate glass. They
had passed a lot of windows, he and his mother on their
first real outing since the hospital, but none so grand as this.

"Mama!" he said. He said it loudly, though she was right
there holding his arm so tight her knuckles glowed white. He
couldn't feel her grip and so forgot her for blocks at a time.

She rustled next to him, stirring up the reassuring scent of vanilla
from the folds in her skirt. "I'm here." She reached to touch his
head, the only part of his upper body that wasn't encased in a
plaster cast that crudely approximated his long john undershirt
at its dirtiest.

But he turned and tipped forward before she could reach him.
For a breathless second, she saw him fall to the sidewalk and crack
like an egg — but his wire collar, protruding in stiff, closely sym-
metrical spokes, caught the wide window ledge and held him until
she managed to right him properly in front of what he wanted to
see. He had given her so many scares that now she brushed her
terror to some unknown place without a second thought.

She had learned how to do that in the hospital after his acci-
dent, sitting beside his iron bed, helpless to watch the doctors
try to still the pain that yawned and screamed across his face.

"Look, Mama," he said now. He tried to point forward, but
the plaster held his arms in a T's crossbar. "Fancy ladies!"

The cast was the last step, the doctors had reassured her. It
would hold all of the bones close enough to heal. The doctor
with the beard spilling down his chest had been most vehement
about six weeks' bed rest.

"Do you understand?" He had squinted up at her rather more closely than she preferred, but she had been exhausted, and there was a divan already made up for her broken son next to their radiator that he liked to pat when the apartment got cold. She had inclined her head and taken their glass bottles of medicine. Six weeks and one day later, they needed more.

"Mama, can I go?" he had asked like a skipping gramophone, through the morning and the porridge she spooned into his mouth around the words. "Can I go? Can I go?"

But he had slipped away to sleep when she had prepared herself in the afternoon, so she whispered a quick plea to Miss Johnson to watch him while she got the medicine alone. Coming back inside, she had looked at him, trapped in his own body, and she had hidden the shopping bag as she waited for him to open his eyes again.

Staring into the window, he smiled at the fancy ladies. "Mama, they look like you."

The fancy ladies didn't move. Their smiles were painted on and their joints were stiff. An extra leg with its boot and knee stocking freshened stood by. As they watched, she savoring the bit of breeze biting at her chin and he in expectation of movement, a rectangle opened in the wall behind the fancy ladies.

The fancy ladies remained still as a young man in coveralls climbed into their window and produced a screwdriver. A few practiced turns of the tool dismantled the fancy ladies, who lay scattered without protest along the deep red carpet of their home.

The boy's mother colored a bit in her cheeks and had a vague sense she should protect him from — what? Something was vulgar about this, but before she could think of what, the young man had screwed everyone back together again.

"He fixed them." Her boy tried to clap. The young man saw and made one of the fancy ladies wave her hand before he disappeared through the back wall of the window.

"They're fixed," she said, leaning down to take his plastered hand. He threw the fancy ladies one last look before letting his mother lead him home.

Fries with That

Rebecca Waddell

Hunger drives my swollen feet forward. I'm craving fries. As the restaurant doors open, the delicious aroma ensnares me, pulling me inside. My stomach cramps in anticipation, or maybe the baby just kicked. Either way, I smile as I order a generous serving of the salty, potatoey goodness. "Extra large fries please."

Behind me, two women in their forties are discussing what to get. I pay and shift my ever expanding bulk out of their way. Instead of moving straight up to the counter to order, they look me up and down like I'm some kind of side show. My fry fixation is interrupted as I wonder how they will react to my teen pregnancy.

Twenty minutes ago at the bank, a woman sneered at me. Last week, a lady in the bathroom started to congratulate me on my condition, until she saw my face. Without make-up on, I look fifteen, not seventeen. The judgment that filled her eyes was instantaneous: I was too young to be pregnant. I see the same look growing in the taller woman's eyes.

The second woman gives me a small smile, like Mandy from church did when she first saw my pregnancy. After the smile, she invited me to lunch. I've come to treasure the few who react like her. As the tall woman draws in enough breath for a long rant, I hope she isn't like the woman in the grocery store. With four little ones trailing behind her, she lectured me for five minutes straight about how stupid I was to get pregnant at my age. I've grown a thick skin against people like her. They don't know I didn't choose this path or my condition.

The taller woman releases a long sigh, leans toward her friend, and mutters, "Oh look, another pregnant teen. Our welfare system at work." The second woman smirks but tries to hide it.

My face burns. I'm used to these remarks. Most of the time I don't let them get to me. Maybe it's the pregnancy hormones, but then I have to say something. I flash a smile. "Excuse me. What gives you the right to judge me?" I ask in an unassuming voice.

"I'm sure your parents will help you. Anyway, I pay taxes. I shouldn't have to pay for the trouble you got yourself into," she fires back.

Her friend glances around as if she's looking for a rock to crawl under. My smile widens. "You know, you're right. I should've gone against my religious convictions and personal morals and gotten an abortion so I wouldn't be a drain on society."

Their mouths hang open. "I never said that!" defends the tall woman. Her friend takes a step toward the bathroom. "You have a lot of nerve preaching morality, young lady," she argues.

I laugh. This is absurd. "If only you knew what you were talking about," I reply, shaking my head.

"Oh, really? Why don't you enlighten me then?" she asks.

Her friend takes another step and looks on the verge of running. I feel bad for the friend. "I didn't get pregnant on purpose," I say quietly.

The woman waves her hand dismissively. "Of course not, but birth control does fail," she chastises.

"Yes, and some people were virgins before they got raped," I reply.

A loud bang comes from the bathroom door as the friend slips through it. Silence follows. I hold the tall woman's gaze for the fifteen long seconds that the quiet remains unbroken. I will her to continue her rant.

"Number eighty-five," calls an employee.

"That's me!" I announce and break the eye contact. Fries in hand, I leave the woman standing speechless in the middle of the restaurant. These are the best fries I've ever tasted.

Sudden Horripilation

Chella Courington

In a green tunic the barefoot man held the smoke in his hands and rubbed it over their shoes and jeans, chests and faces.

"Sage will protect you," the man muttered and turned to the next couple.

"What now?" Tom asked.

"We wait for the guide," Adele said.

They were deep in the Funk Zone, Santa Barbara's Left Bank.

"To broaden our awareness of how we fill physical space," she said.

Tom, who had apologized for his last movie choice three times, deferred.

"I already know. You're 5'9", weigh 159; I'm 5'11", weighed 200," he said

She didn't smile.

Through a yin yang beaded curtain, the guide led them up a narrow staircase to a black room, two women in tights suspended on aerial cables. No music, no voice, a white light on black encased muscle and bone twisting around thick wire, arms pulling the other closer until torsos and heads melded, energy flowing through them like a circuit with no breaker. Adele's right hand touched Tom's, vessels raised and soft. With the tip of her forefinger, she traced the longest from his wrist over bone through knuckles to the base of his middle finger.

She remembered the sudden horripilation traveling up her arms in freshman biology when the instructor lifted his hand and said: "Look at your fingertips. They are more sensitive than your penis or clitoris." She'd felt warm and wet, sucking on her middle finger to test the correlation and understood that masturbation would be the ultimate sexual sensation and that her fingers must be kept clean and moisturized for moments like this when standing together in public, witnessing the foreplay of two bodies on wire, their heat rising, filling the room with musk and yearning so that now Adele turned to Tom, her fingertips teaching his veins to follow her out of the room, down the narrow stairs and past the barefoot man in green to a dark place under the night.

Perfection
("This One")

MaryEllen Baizley

The attendant releases three possible pets into the Greeting Room. I feel drawn to the black female, a short haired and sleek beauty. A small, powerful animal, it literally glides around the room. Despite the chipped white paint and the smell of cat urine, the feline's prowling makes the matted floors seem like the lair of a gorgeous, fearsome panther.

Am I imagining it, or do its sharp green eyes never leave mine? I need this cat. It is not the kind of cat that you adopt. It's the kind of cat that adopts you.

"What do you think of..." I start to ask and then wait. Dianne is still looking around the room with wide eyes.

"So cute! How do we decide?" Dianne asks. "I wish Jackie could help me pick one."

I put a hand on Dianne's forearm. Recuperating at home since her latest hospitalization, her BFF Jackie will live the experience vicariously through Dianne's photos and texts. Jackie's replies will be full of acronyms and smiley faces.

The jungle panther skates away into the corner. Then a second cat approaches. My daughter exclaims over how cute the cat's fur is — orange with black patches. It nudges its head against us and jumps up onto Dianne's knees. I touch it, and its fur feels soft in my fingers.

"I think they call this kind a money cat, is that right?" I ask.

My daughter shrugs, petting her fluffy new friend.

She snaps a quick picture of its orangey face with her cell phone.

The Humane Society attendant bustles back into the room. Her green name tag reads "Mrs. Shay" in white lettering. "How's it going in here, ladies?" she asks. "I see you met Oscar. Shadow is also a great choice. Which of those two would you like?"

"This one. What about this one?" Dianne asks. She points to a third cat, still curled up on the exact spot where Mrs. Shay had placed her. The cat sits and watches us with intense green eyes. From across the room, I can see that there is a visibly shaved patch on its side and under its belly.

"Surgery?" I ask.

Mrs. Shay nods.

When Dianne picks the gray, striped cat up, it flinches a bit, then settles in and dozes in her arms. Dianne stares into its half-opened, oval green eyes. Soon Oscar the orange cat is following Dianne and rubbing against her ankles, but she doesn't notice.

"What's the gray cat's name?" I ask.

Mrs. Shay clears her throat and says, "That cat's name is Jade, and she needs a life-long home. She was a stray that a good Samaritan brought in, after the cat was hit by a car in Lewiston. Terrible! Jade's hip was broken, and she had internal injuries. She had to undergo emergency surgery."

"You'll be better soon," Dianne coos at Jade in her arms. Jade's ears perk up at the mention of her name.

"She's sick, and she'll be sick for a while," Mrs. Shay cautions. "Dr. Kleiner, our vet, says that she will require a lot of care as she recovers. She will need to stay inside for a while. Her injuries prevent her from avoiding predators like fisher cats and coyotes."

Mrs. Shay pauses. She raises an eyebrow and looks at me. I move closer to Dianne and pet Jade's downy head. Jade purrs.

"Although Dr. K anticipates she will soon regain the ability to walk, she would need to be carried up and down the stairs for a while."

Jade mews and Dianne draws her mouth into a line.

"I can carry her," she says.

"I would love nothing more than to find Jade a nice owner like you, but sometimes when families adopt sick cats, they can't handle the care and then they bring them back. I don't want that to happen to Jade," Mrs. Shay says.

"I would never do that!" Dianne walks away from Mrs. Shay and me, still cradling Jade in her arms.

"She will require frequent vet follow-up visits. You understand that, Mom?" Mrs. Shay asks.

"Yes," I say, as dollar signs dart through my brain.

"The doctors predict she will always walk with a limp," Mrs. Shay continues.

"She's perfect," Dianne says, snapping a picture of the blinking cat with her phone. "Perfect! I can't wait to tell Jackie! Where do we sign?"

As we head out to the car, Dianne walks in front of me lugging a plastic cat carrier in one hand and her cell phone in the other. Mild Maine sunshine dances around us. Tall blue lupines ring the parking lot.

"I couldn't believe it," Dianne tells Jackie, who lies propped up on a pink pillow in her bedroom with polka-dot wallpaper, wincing from the pain of inherited scoliosis. "Like, they are supposed to find families for the cats but the lady tried to talk me out of taking the best one. Oh my God! Wait 'til you see my kitty!"

As we near our white minivan, I watch my no-longer-little girl veer over toward the passenger side. I see once again how her left leg, having been broken twice when she was a toddler, has never properly healed. Her left leg remains slightly shorter than her right. As she walks in her silver flip flops, her leg bows out and gives her a hint of a limp.

I dig into my black purse for my keys. Small drops of warm rain begin to fall softly on our cheeks and hands.

Dianne pulls the cat carrier closer to her body. "Don't worry kitty, I'll keep you dry."

"She's perfect," I say.

My daughter rocks the car carrier back and forth, whispering to Jade. Smiling, I open the passenger side door and beckon the new friends inside.

III

Our Possible Futures

"Ambient Temperature" by Coelynn McIninch

Third Serving

Barbara Baer

I'd skyped Sita in Mumbai. "We've banquet seats for our wedding supper." Her lovely, covered head nodded side to side, our Indian way of saying yes. Then she placed five slim fingers on the screen as if to touch my face. My heart flip-flopped with thoughts of intimacies to come.

When her plane finally landed and tired passengers emerged, I tried not to feel disappointment seeing the stick of a girl, the tip of her sari covering her face. According to her father, Sita was twenty-five but her body looked like a child beneath the folds of cloth. I should have been prepared. In India they'd been starving for three generations while we'd only been hard-pressed for two. Ages could no longer be guessed. We all looked younger or older than our ages since we carried no excess flesh. The bones of our ancestors showed in our faces and like them, we didn't reach ages achieved by our grandparents. Fifty was considered old age.

I pedaled as fast as I could to reach home, where I made her herbal tea and biscuits before chastely leading her to bed. As I watched her sleep, she seemed to dream constantly, her dark eyelashes quivering on her olive skin, her limbs pressed together as if she were still in the constricted position of the plane. I felt compassion more than anything, though I believed that love would come with time. It's been proven that couples have a greater will to survive than singles. Altruism added years to your life.

Our wedding was at six. Sita dressed in a beautiful red sari and wound her braid into a chignon. My heart flip-flopped at her womanliness, but when she raised her arms to attach a stray curl, ribs and hip bones gleamed white.

Following the group marriage ceremony, we walked with other newlyweds to the Biltmore Hotel where First Serving was still in progress, and the line for Second went around the block. Three years ago, Father and I had Second Serving after Mother's death. I remembered leading Father into the hall, where the maitre d' seated us and the waiters bowed above fine china. Ladies wore wildflower corsages but the hunger pains in our stomach were so great we barely glanced at the crystal. We ate until the closing bell rang.

Father passed on a few weeks later, his skeletal hand in mine.

Sita was also grieving for her father. Vijay's last act had been to find me, a distant cousin on Mother's side, living in Los Angeles. Vijay assured me that apart from malnutrition, Sita's health was good. We settled marriage plans. He'd put his last strength into writing, "Sita's a good pure girl, Sashi. She never fights for scraps."

"She won't have to," I replied. "I shall provide."

In the weeks leading up to Sita's arrival, I pedaled longer hours and used less of my rations than ever.

I now touched Sita's arm. "We'll be called soon. Third Serving is in some respects preferable, my dearest. We won't be rushed. I remember when scarcity began in California we used to pool our foods in neighborhood dinners called pot luck."

"Pot luck? Was it Chinese?" Her sweet face tilted toward me, and our eyes met.

"American, possibly a native custom. Everyone brought a dish from home and ate from a common platter, as we shall do at Third Serving."

"Father told me about his wedding day. So many sweets you couldn't possibly eat all. The way he described milk sweets and the gulab jamun, I almost felt I was tasting and swallowing. Sweets I am missing most of all."

At the barrier cord, I shielded Sita from watching staff pile Second's plates onto platters for us. I've heard that sometimes they add more from the kitchen. We might be pot-lucky this evening.

"Just married," I said to a Eurasian family seated beside Sita, hoping they'd make her feel at ease, but their eyes saw nothing except the platters. On my side, a gaunt pair sat so lightly it was as if they'd lived on air, which perhaps they'd learned to do on a Penance Farm. Third Servings often honored the recently released.

As soon as they gave permission to fill our plates, I couldn't help myself from forking up and masticating purposefully to allow stomach juices to rise and prolong sensations of fullness in the mouth. In those moments when the belly was no longer crying out, one could become reflective about life as our Wise Ones suggested we do until the situation improved.

I reached across and placed brownish lumps on Sita's plate. When she didn't move to take any, I picked up a dripping brown morsel and brought it to her lips. Still she didn't eat. This was hardly a time to lecture her on the necessities of protein for survival — Sita is from the Brahmin caste, as I am — but she had to eat, because I had nothing at home.

The ravaged woman beside me rapped lightly on my shoulder and slipped a piece of chocolate into Sita's hand. Chocolate! Where had she obtained chocolate?

"Thank you, Missus," I said. "Thank you."

My bride shyly accepted her gift, placed the square in her mouth and sucked slowly, her cheeks drawn in, her eyes closed, as if tasting the world in this square of sweetness. She never fought for scraps, her father had said.

Station 352A

Wendy Nikel

Seventeen space-kliks out, a light blinked over a battered sign. "Danger: Asteroids." Beneath it, as an afterthought, was another sign: "Refueling Station Ahead."

On a clear day, when the asteroids were off bothering someone else and Station 352A's water system hadn't fogged up the windows, I could watch it. On. Off. On. Off. I'd stare at it for hours. It was usually more interesting than the single vid station I could get out here. Not much else a girl could do so far out in no man's land.

Some days, another light would brighten my sky. A spaceship. As soon as I'd spot it, I'd stream around the refueling station, wiping glass and straightening freeze-dried snacks on the displays as if I hadn't done the same thing each morning since I'd taken up my post here.

Today's ship was a sleek, military two-seater, pockmarked with dents. Good news and bad news. Dents meant that its pilot might actually get out and chat while the station's droid repaired the ship. However, such a fancy craft probably carried an officer, and they tended to be wound too tightly for jawing with a lowly refuel stationer, especially right after being pummeled by asteroids.

Tether secured, I floated out to the ship's hatch. "Fuel or just repairs?" I asked, clicking on the short-distance com system.

The hatch hissed open and a portly man emerged. Despite his spotless helmet, it was obvious that the war hadn't treated him well. He'd lost an eye, and the skin around the socket fell inward like a sinkhole. I tried to hide my shudder.

"Both," he said gruffly. "Hurry it up, miss. I'm on military business."

I chuckled and pulled out the fuel hose. "Aren't we all?"

The officer scoffed. Wasn't the first time I dealt with attitude like his. They played with their lasers while I played connect-the-star-dots with washable marker on the station's windows, but we'd both been drafted into this pointless war. Trouble was, most military felt their job of using up resources was more important than my job of providing them. No use arguing. Not like they'd listen.

"There," I said an hour later, when the droid's lights blinked green. "All set."

"About time," he grumbled, heaving himself up from my armchair and snapping his helmet on. He stepped into the airlock. I shrugged, letting him go without a farewell. The silence of two people trying not to converse is always more silent than the silence of one person alone. And, no, the droid doesn't count.

With Captain Craterface gone, I dimmed the lights and lay on my cot, gazing at the stars. It wasn't bunktime yet, at least not by military time, but my time was my own, and the occasional nap helped stem my boredom.

The light of the officer's shuttle disappeared, and I entertained myself by watching the warning sign's light. On. Off. On. Off.

Another light. The officer must have forgotten something. No, this light was different. Two shuttles in one day? What were the chances?

Shining up the station seemed pointless, having just done so an hour ago, so I donned my suit, tethered myself to the dock, and waited. I clung to the edge, but my feet hung down into the great nothingness of space. A vague recollection of summers on a wooden pier, with feet dipped in crisp, cool water flitted through my mind, but I couldn't recall if that was something I'd actually done or just something I'd seen on the vids. My childhood on Earth had become a half-remembered dream.

I was still staring into the bottomless lake of the universe when the shuttle docked. It was an older model, and as beat up as the surface of a moon.

"Whoo!" I said. "You must have hit a particularly vengeful patch of 'roids out there."

The hatch hissed open and the ship's pilot grinned. "You might say that."

He was younger than most, making me question how he'd survived this long. Most men of my generation had been wiped out in the first decade of fighting. His face was scarred, and he walked with a limp, so I assumed he'd been one of the "lucky ones" sent home early with injuries. Their luck wore off a few years later when injured veterans were included in subsequent drafts, but at least they got to enjoy a few years of their youth.

"Just fuel," he said, winking.

"Just fuel?" I started the pump. "Hate to say it, but your ship's a mess. You ought to get it repaired. My droid here's pretty good—"

He shook his head. "Just fuel. I can't afford to stop."

He looked about nervously, and it all clicked into place.

"You're a deserter."

"Officially, I'm dead," he said, shrugging, "and my ship destroyed. Now if you use that droid of yours on it, though, someone might discover it's a little less destroyed than they assumed. We wouldn't want that."

I crossed my arms, studying him. He wasn't like anyone I'd seen in all the years I'd been stuck here. Most were either hyper-focused and hardened, or beat-down and tired. Here was someone who looked...alive.

"All right," I said. "What's in it for me? I'm risking my livelihood here, you know."

"You mean this job?" When I nodded, a smile played out over his face. "What do you need this job for? Come with me."

I balked, but his face was hopeful, sincere. How long had I been here, anyway? How much of my life had been spent killing time, waiting, hoping someone would show up just so I'd have someone to talk to? He raised his eyebrows, daring, pleading me to say yes.

The pump's light blinked green. The tank was full. I looked over my shoulder at my station, at my perfectly-aligned rows of freeze-dried snacks and my cot that looked into the heavens. Then I looked at the pilot and at his smile made crooked by scars.

"All right. Let's go."

Time Machine

Melissa Webster

She read about the time machine in *National Geographic*. It was a French scientist working at a university in Toronto. The article took a slightly sardonic tone, as though the writer was eager to convey that everyone thought this guy a bit of a nutter. The scientist in question had struggled to get funding for years. Bankrupted himself. His wife left him. He'd been working on it for 10 years.

He wasn't trying to go back in time in the usual way. Just back into earlier parts of his own life. To take his current consciousness back to his younger body and younger life. That's what got her attention.

It took her six months to sell the house and all her possessions, to pay off her debt, and buy a plane ticket. She had a bit left over to live on for a while. It was all she would need.

At first he didn't see how serious she was.

"You know I haven't figured out a way to come back yet," he said.

"That's okay," she said.

"And it's very likely you won't survive the first transfer anyway," he said.

"It's fine," she said.

"If you do survive the transfer, I don't know how long you'll survive on the other side."

"I know," she said. "I've read all your reports."

"I know you need a subject. To test it."

Eventually he agreed. He made her write to her family to explain her choice. It was a condition that she commit it to writing.

She promised she would. She wrote a letter to her mother that said: "I'm going back to get my baby." She left it with her will, and the instructions to cremate the body she would be leaving behind.

She signed everything the scientist's lawyers wanted. She had only one condition: that she get to decide the exact destination time, down to the minute.

He sedated her for the transfer, to protect her system from shock, and she woke up in the labor room.

The labor was easier than she remembered. Perhaps because this time she knew how it would turn out. She experienced every contraction like a revelation.

The only thing that shook her was when she noticed her very young mother, beside the bed, smiling encouragingly. She'd forgotten her mother was ever that young.

The baby was crying heartily, and her tired body ached to hold him.

"Why don't you just let the nurses clean him up, honey," her mother said.

But the girl was strong. "No," she said. "I want to hold him first."

The warm, slippery, little body was placed over her soft empty belly, and it reached up and snuffled towards her breasts, seeking out a nipple.

"Mother, would you please go get me a soda?" she said then, and when she was alone she took the stained sheet from the bed, and wrapped it around herself and her baby, pressing him against her, and then walked stiffly, painfully down a long, cold, white corridor, until she found a way out. Nobody tried to stop her. She went into the gardens, under a bright sun, and started towards a bench in a far corner, beneath a big lone tree. It was warm out. He would be fine. They would be found soon enough, if it came to that.

She saw the adoption lady then, the social worker, arriving in a rush, bustling into the hospital, carrying files, talking on a cell.

She was already feeling a bit sick, weak, but it might just be from the birth. She was losing blood. It dripped down her legs as she walked over the densely green and yielding lawn. She slumped onto the bench. The tree was a great old oak. It spread its arms over them and rustled quietly.

They found them within twenty minutes. She was already dead. Lying on her side on the bench, covered by the sheet. When they lifted the white cotton, he was curled up against her. Small and pink and perfect, with sticky black hair. The nipple had slipped from his mouth, and he was asleep.

Happy Planet Nursery

Tara Campbell

Ladies and gentleman, welcome to Happy Planet Nursery. You have been selected for a very special mission: to provide the best of care for the children of the brave members of our fine Pan-Galactic Forces. For your next two years on this ship, you will bear the immense responsibility of caring for the offspring of the courageous soldiers who protect our galaxies.

You've all been through rigorous instruction on your planets, but there is no substitute for actual hands-on work, which is where I come in. My name is Nanny O'Brien, and I have the privilege of guiding you through the next two weeks of on-site training. At the end of these two weeks, you will be responsible for the wellbeing of over 1,000 infants and children of various races, places, makes, marks, breeds, and creeds on board.

We will start with a tour of the facilities. We are standing in the playroom, into which dozens of toddlers will swarm after their morning feeding. Space is a little tight, and the word "swarm" is not just figurative, so prepare yourselves. It's quiet now, but you will soon be responsible for settling any number of territorial disputes over playthings visible and invisible, tangible and intangible, make-believe and real. Adjudicate wisely and with justice.

Now, ladies and gentleman, follow me, and I will show you the feeding room. This is for the older ones who can sit up, lie down, or levitate on their own while eating. The little tykes can sit/lie/levitate anywhere they like, but they get their food from different stations. Most of the children pick it up pretty quickly and know where to go, but you have to watch out for the new ones.

I know you've all had your species biology, good old spec-bo — I hated spec-bo — but don't worry if you forget some of the finer points. We have a list by each station of which life-forms should be feeding where. Carbon-based over here, silicon-based here, nitrogen- and arsenic-based over here and here. My favorite is the phosphorous-based food, all pretty and sparkly. 'Course it ain't so pretty coming out the other end...

Which brings us to everyone's least favorite part of the tour — the changing stations. Respirator masks are at the door, and everyone should put one on before they go in. Not every species requires this, but it's a good habit to get into as you enter this chamber. As you can see, we have tables of different varieties: flat, round, synthetic, organic, magnetic, antiseptic, parabolic, hyperbolic, concave, convex, complex, and underwater changing stations for this most arduous of tasks. Please consult the chart on the wall for those species whose feces must be disposed of in the biohazard bin. This is very important, so please repeat after me: I will not misplace the waste! Very good.

And now, ladies and gentleman, on to the infants' chamber. We like to end the tour on an up note.

As you see, we have different beds and burrows, pods and pools, webs and warrens for different kinds of children. The infants have various sleeping and feeding patterns, so we have to monitor the room to keep them from waking each other up too frequently.

You may have noticed by now that there are no Sploozians here. Have any of you ever dealt with a Sploozian child? No? These are ones to watch for. We do not keep them with the other children. As I'm sure you've been told, they are eating machines, and if they don't see you coming WITH food, they will see you AS food.

Over in this corner we have several simulation infants. Let's all come over here and start working with the dummies before you start working with the real thing.

Just fan out and find a child, that's it.

Nice work, Malia, that's one happy little guy you've got. Keep it up!

Gesundheit, Louise. Are you allergic to feathered children? We've got pills for that.

June, if that had been a real Frenian you would have been vaporized by now. Did you realize you were picking it up by its head? I can guarantee that child would have, and it would have chosen a highly eternal way of making you aware of that.

And Norman? Norman? Where's Norman?

Jesus H. Chronos, Marie, what are you doing to that child? You call that feeding? Your technique wouldn't even be acceptable in the brig! Nobody waterboards anymore, not even on Earth. Here, watch. See, just very small drops of water, that's it.

Congratulations, Andrea, you almost got yourself blown up. Never squeeze a Jovian baby that hard. I don't care how cute it is!

And Norman? All right, where the hell is he? Norman, what are you doing up there? Ladies, help me cut him out of this cocoon. The escape kit is over here. I keep telling Command they should separate the training area from the rest of the nursery, but they never listen to me. They all forget so much.

All right Norman, dust yourself off and find a practice infant. No rest for us. The babies of Happy Planet Nursery never take a holiday, so neither can we. Once you make it through here, you'll have a set of skills that can take you to the highest levels of Command. I've trained 'em all — Commander Druvinian, Andrews, Bleckman — they've all been through nursery duty.

But me, I'm not going anywhere. The children need me here. And I continue to hope that some of you, once you get to the top, will manage to remember the lessons this place teaches you: share your toys, learn something every day, and don't bite off the head that feeds you.

Now, if you'll — what's that noise? Holy gargantuan, who let the Sploozian child out? Ladies and gentleman, stand back. Somebody get me a steak from the feeding room. Here's how I earn MY stripes.

Orange Sky Preparation

Mardra Sikora

The first month the old woman didn't pay her rent, she bought a gun instead. The next month she ordered a live lobster. A boy brought it in a box strapped to the back of his bike. She handed him a two-dollar coin. Then they both turned and stood a moment, watching her neighbors shuffle their crying children into an overstuffed car. She shrugged and plucked a single envelope from her mailbox. The boy raced off.

Her other neighbors had left last night with only one suitcase each. He'd put the bags in the trunk while she'd pulled on the locked door three times to make sure it stuck. Perhaps they had felt her watching them from the window, because they'd never looked her way. She wondered why they even owned a house along the beach, both soft and white like cotton balls. Never saw them in anything but long pants and sun hats.

"The winds are coming, it's true, but everyone is afraid of the wrong storm," she thought.

Years of salty air and windblown sand took the paint off her house as well as the softness from her skin, coloring them both brown and weathered.

Once her sons had left for the war, she too had packed up only one suitcase and come here to the ocean. Even though she'd known their fates when they left, she'd let them go anyway, waving goodbye with a proud smile.

When they didn't return, a reporter called her to research "a story of sacrifice." He wanted to portray her patriotic spirit, so she told him to fuck off.

In her time, she kept a small garden, walked the shore, and ate alone as some kind of warning. She lived as a silent beacon of aging loneliness.

When her latest vision came so clearly in the night — the mushroom cloud on the orange sky horizon — she again kept it to herself. She shook the image away and picked up the box from the porch.

"They can all try to run," she told her scuttling captive while she carried the box to the kitchen and then opened the top. She filled the pot and turned on the stove. "I bought some real salted butter, too." Then she pulled a bottle out from under the sink and took a cloth over the sandy dust it collected. "Scotch," she told the lobster. "Good stuff. Haven't had any for a long time."

She perched over the pot to see the bubbles just beginning, moved to gather a short glass, and then poured the copper liquid. The first swallow made her wince. "Good stuff," she proclaimed again and set down the glass with a slight bang on the table. "Okay buddy, your time is up." The lobster plopped into the rolling boil, and the air wailed from its shell.

She set a timer on the stove, collected the envelope from the table, and went outside. She sat in her favorite spot on the porch, the salty air sticking to her skin. The incoming storm blew sand across her bare feet.

The crisp envelope bent beneath her fingers as she laid it on her lap. She was surprised, amused really, that the eviction notice arrived. "Why did they bother?" she mused aloud. "Probably all automated. Idiots."

She pulled a pen from her dress pocket and wrote *Go to Hell* on the envelope and *Return to Sender,* then tossed it over the porch edge and watched the wind catch and glide it out over the waves. She shook her head, went back into the house, and loaded her gun.

The weatherman warned of the hurricane winds. But it was that crazy bastard from across the ocean that would bring the storm tonight. If her vision was correct — and her visions always were — there was enough time to enjoy her dinner and another glass of scotch before the first cloud formed up from the earth and melted away the distant horizon.

Made For This

Amanda Larson

A draft blew over her bare skin as she stood in line. Bright lights left nowhere for even the smallest wrinkle to hide. Pulsing music spilled in from the club, shaking the sterile walls of the evaluation room and jarring her nerves.

A dozen other women also awaited their weekly inspection. Before they left the womb, the world knew what they would look like and what they would become.

Sometimes, even that wasn't enough.

One of the new girls had already been taken away. She was pregnant when they were supposed to be sterile. Her replacement was on order.

The raven-haired woman behind her stood next to a replacement. They were identical except the new girl was ten years younger. Only one would clear inspection.

They all took their turn on the scale. When it was hers, she brushed aside her blond locks and held out her wrist to be scanned. They were only numbers, all sharing the same names.

Bitch. Slut. Whore.

The club's manager looked at his assistant. "When's that blond replacement due?"

"Tomorrow."

The manager pushed her forward. No inspection. No need. They were done with her.

She stumbled off the scale, slipped into her panties, and latched her bra with unsteady fingers. She tried not to hear the other woman's pleas, which tomorrow could be her own.

They all knew there was nothing after this.

The air was heavy with sweat, sex, and liquor, tightening her chest further as she stepped through the door to start her show. There wasn't anything else to do. This was all she'd ever known.

The crowd hollered as she swung around the nearest pole. Her strength, endurance, and rhythm were all built in. All still there.

She'd done nothing wrong. Her body wasn't failing. She'd be replaced because of a calendar date.

No one would even notice.

Her replacement would already know the poles and how to move her lips when she dropped to her knees. She'd have been told that men would worship her, not that they'd leave her bloody and sore.

Just one more night.

She unfurled from the ground and strutted along the stage. Greedy hands grappled for her legs as she passed. State law said the choice of who to have was hers. The club agreed as long as she filled her nightly quota.

Tonight quotas didn't matter. They'd already marked her as trash. Tonight she'd take her time.

She found the one surrounded by empty shot glasses. He was a short, scrawny man bundled in a jacket with the hood masking his face. This look was typical among high-profile clients of whom no questions were asked.

She slid off the stage to stand in front of him, blocking his view of the black-haired girl that held his gaze.

"You're not my type," he said.

"Really? Because you're just what I need."

She had his attention. They always settled for the one in reach. One body was as good as another.

Sliding down onto his lap sealed the deal. His hands clutched her curves, not that they'd ever really been hers.

She arched into him until she knew she had him then sauntered towards the nearest private room. She didn't look back. They always followed.

She'd spent her life in these dimly lit rooms, with only a bed and toys for those who liked to play.

The door clanked shut and the man shoved his hand beneath the strap of her g-string. She backed him into the wall, pressing in until the stench of bourbon stung her eyes.

Soon she had him stripped on the bed. Her teeth teased sensitive skin as she guided his arms to the restraints.

Familiar names slid from his lips. She smiled to herself as she bound his wrists. He was the one panting like a whore.

She leaned in to kiss his breath away. He lifted his head to push his bitter tongue in further while she slipped the pillow from beneath his head.

He moaned through clenched teeth as her hips ground over his. She didn't keep him waiting.

His eyes closed, and she pressed the pillow over his face. It could have been any man. All of them. She used the strength they'd given her to hold the pillow until the body went limp.

They'd taught her to be what she had to be. She followed her lessons, changing as quickly she had between any group of men.

The clothes she claimed felt heavy against her skin. She welcomed the foreign sensation and pulled the hood over her head as she left the room for the last time.

She must have been made for more than this.

Mars Whimpering

Mary Finnegan

The sun is shining, and the air holds the thick aroma of roses. Savannah is one with Rocket, a magnificent black steed, as they jump over the ten foot high rock fence and land inside a beautiful garden where colors are indescribable in reality. Everything here is more real than real.

At once, Savannah and Rocket are surrounded by loved ones beaming their pleasure: Her lover, her soul mate, Ricardo, is darkly handsome like Rocket — he and Rocket share a soul, she imagines. Her dad is there. Her mother! Her child, laughing and clapping. Even the dog rushes to her as she dismounts. They are all perfect. So is she.

BEEP. BEEP.

It takes a moment for Savannah to realize she is being called back to reality. Reality? What is that?

It is Domenick, invading her private space, her capsule. She comes from full-immersion virtual reality to real reality: her surroundings are drab, totally depressing. She is taken by the thought that Domenick is dark, tall, very handsome, and her virtual reality lover, Ricardo, greatly resembles him. But Ricardo is much more vibrant.

"What do you want?" she snaps. She clings to her memories of virtual reality like an addiction. "Why can't you just leave me alone?"

Domenick is sweating, breathing hard. "Listen," he says. His eyes linger on her. Moments ago, he'd been having sex with her in full-immersion virtual reality, but she didn't know that. He takes a deep breath. "We've found life here on Mars!"

She sits, not because she really feels the impact of his words, but shock at this news is expected of her. If she is real. "Actually," she says between clinched teeth, "discovering life is not what we were sent here for."

Domenick shrugs. "These things happen."

He sits facing her. "While we were drilling to find more space for humanity to expand — I don't know how many feet down, hundreds, maybe thousands — we broke into a chamber. Containing a life form. And then, others. Other chambers, containing life forms!"

Shadows enclosed the two like a womb.

"And what do these chambers look like?" she asked.

"Well, like this. Like your capsule. Like mine. I mean, all capsules look alike."

"And these life forms. What do they look like?"

"Human. Like me." He takes a deep breath. "Like you."

Domenick led the female into Savannah's capsule and then made a quick exit. Females were better at feelings and communication, he reasoned.

Savannah saw a human much like herself: small female, long dark tangled hair, blue eyes fringed in dark lashes, full lips. They sat facing each other, eyes fixed.

"My name is Savannah."

"No name," said the other.

"Please explain."

"Why did you dig me up?" The other asked all in one breath. "Why did you remove me from my reality? Why can't you just leave me alone?"

Savannah reached way inside herself to remember humans. She pointed at herself. "My life form, human, came from Earth," she stammered. "Our planet, Earth, was a garden. A place of trees, oceans, animals." Although she had no real memory of those things.

"So was Mars," said her mirror image, holding direct her stare.

"When we were totally human, we had wars and class-states. Little children starving to death. Weapons of mass destruction. At least the world didn't end with a bang. We didn't blow ourselves up! We became symbiotic with machines. We lived forever. And we have full-immersion virtual reality!"

"Your world ended with a whimper, as did mine."

"Technology kept us alive, even as the planet died."

The other nodded. "I understand. This also happened with the life forms here on Mars."

"When the earth died, and there were no oceans or vegetation or animals, and Mother Earth could no longer sustain the trillions of human life-forms, an invention saved us. We called it the eternal, internal combustion machine." Savannah gave a laugh, and it was strange to her. She didn't think she had ever before laughed.

Dimly, she recalled her last real meal: steak, a salad, and dark chocolate ice cream.

The other smiled awkwardly. "I know! I understand!" She giggled then seemed startled at her own impulsiveness. "We also became human-machines. We live forever! We recycle our own waste!"

"Right! And we have full-immersion virtual reality, so once we lived forever, and the planet was dead, all we needed was more room!"

"I know! You each have a capsule. You don't need anything else!"

"Well, we did. We needed more room. That's why we came here to Mars. And then, after we covered the surface of this planet, we dug underground."

"So did we! And then you came and disturbed us!"

For long moments, their eyes met in a dark communication.

Then Savannah's opposite said in a strangled voice, "We buried ourselves with our entertainment systems."

Savannah studied her mirror image, so much like her own face, whose skin now seemed to become white, then transparent, a skull with exposed white teeth. The jaw moved, exposing eternal darkness inside the skull. "I had a child," she said in a horrible voice.

As if it was information encoded in her junk DNA, Savannah remembered. She also had a child.

Really.

She reached a hand to touch this other self, a mother.

"Don't!" Instinctively the other pulled back with her hand raised in warning.

Savannah took a sharp intake of breath. This was real.

"Now I'm going back to my capsule. My virtual reality."

Tears flowed from Savannah's eyes. She had never cried, or if she had, she didn't recall when. She told herself, I'll remember this, this real. But all she could manage to say to the other was, "We'll leave you alone."

Savannah was one with the black stallion. They leaped the ten-foot rock fence into the garden, where her lover and her child awaited her.

Prime Numbers

Melissa J. Lytton

I am two and there is a whale in the sky. It doesn't make any noise, but every time it eats a star, all the big people scream together, like mice.

I am three and we live in the desert. Crawling on bellies to a new home. A flat place full of snakes.

I am five and we live in the ice. I wake up with blue toes every morning. If I can't feel the ground, how will I grow taller?

I am seven and we live in a b-u-i-l-d-i-n-g. The floor is smooth and cold like home. No crawling allowed, little missy.

I am seven and I am choosing the wrong side, dammit! What's wrong with you? She's just a kid. They'll tear her to pieces like crumbling salt.

I am seven. I got to see a flower today. No one is happy. The aliens like flowers, too. Their bodies smell like earth.

I am not eight. I will never be eight. I am seven, I am seven, I am seven-seven-seven-seven, and I want to see the flower again.

No one is happy here.

The aliens like my flower.

I am twenty-three. I will give you all my flowers for a different kind of green. There are no more stars to eat, and the snakes are all dead. My toes still burn at night when he warms them up. Blood will always betray you like that.

All my flowers for your last star.

I am eight and there is a whale in the sky.

I am twenty-nine and there are no more stars to eat.

All the grown-ups scream together.

Blind mice on a battlefield.

IV

Our Dreams;
Our Nightmares

"Ode to Georgia O" by Lisa Lutwyche

Superfluity of Nuns

Tantra Bensko

Mary moved her hips with her woman-of-the-streets swagger, stuck out one leg, and rested her wrists on her narrow hips.

Q had learned her movements since being given as a child to the nunnery, and lorded that over Mary, who would never be able to be as convincing as her as a Bride of Christ. It's like this, she said, taking Mary's shoulders and scrunching them forward a little. Making her look wider and more baboon-like, less modern. She looks at Martha, who furrows her unibrow and nods greyly.

The only reason you're here, Q, is because your parents didn't think you'd be able to find a man worth a flip, definitely not with the dowry they'd have to pay him so they'd be rid of you. That's the only reason Jesus loves you better than he loves me. But I'll bet I could show him a hell of a lot better time.

They all three picked up their Jesus dolls for the special holy day. The brushed the doll's hair and oiled the skin. They rocked him and sang to him songs of stars and animals, blood and feasts of air.

They heard people on the road, outside their thick, barren walls with no windows, bricked up so they couldn't look out and be seen and distract men into depravity. It was the Protestants, yelling at them about being no better than prostitutes. They were coming with hatchets. They were coming with sledgehammers.

See, Mary, I told the sisters what would happen if they kept letting your kind enter our monastery. They hugged their Jesus dolls to their bosoms. Mary opened up her blouse for Jesus, as the walls began to crumble, in the rectangle where there once was a window when they were trusted to look out of it without making every man want them, no matter how homely they were. They would be mangled raw shortly. Mary put the Jesus doll to her areola, and Q took her mallet she had armed herself with and hit her over the head.

Stung

Hall Jameson

Eleven-year-old Chloe trailed Davy Parker as they hiked beneath the evergreens, the ground littered with pine needles and spongy pale mushrooms. The low bushes tickled her bare ankles as she paused to collect pinecones. She held up her fishing pole to avoid tangling with the reaching boughs. They had caught three white perch, one largemouth bass, and a pickerel in the early morning water. The perch hung from a string tied around Chloe's waist; the pickerel and bass hung from Davy's belt.

"We should make chowder!" Davy yelled over his shoulder.

"Good idea," Chloe said, tucking the pinecones into the pockets of her cargo shorts.

Davy stopped and turned. "What are you going to do with a bunch of pinecones?" he asked, stepping onto a mound of pine needles. His right foot sunk into the turf. Losing his balance, he landed on his butt. Chloe ran to him, dropping her pinecones, but he was laughing, embarrassed. His smile disappeared, shifting to a look of confusion as a handful of dark shapes the size of jellybeans began to mill around his head. At first, Chloe thought they were drops shaken loose from a nearby tree. Then something pelted her forehead with a ferocious buzz, and she squawked in surprise and pain.

Hornets erupted from a hole in the ground next to Davy. They were not yellow and black-striped like the robust bumblebees that puttered around her mother's roses, but dark and bullet-shaped. Chloe squealed, waving her arms, but Davy remained motionless as the hornets struck his neck, face, and bare legs.

"Davy! Get up!"

As if waking from a bad dream, Davy sprung to his feet with a shout. He hurled the tackle box at the swarm, now tripled in size. It surrounded them in a furious cloud as they stumbled toward the lake.

The cold water was both soothing and shocking as she ducked under. She looked at Davy under water, his cheeks puffed up with air, his eyes closed. When her head broke the surface, her skin was on fire.

The hornets left them, not interested in wet, splashing things. Davy stood next to her, gingerly touching his cheeks and chin. She draped her arms over his shoulders and looked at his ruined face. There were welts on his neck, chin, and cheeks, and his right eye was swollen shut. The fish tied to her waist floated on the surface of the water like dead leaves.

He picked up the bass floating near his hip, placed it over the stings on his cheek, and closed his eyes.

"We should make chowder tonight," Chloe said, as they walked back to the lodge.

"Good idea," he whispered, the bass still pressed against his cheek.

How it Feels on the Tongue

Eden Royce

Carla sliced open the ruby red grapefruit along its equator. Ran the sharp serrated blade around the perimeter of the fruit and down to separate each juicy segment from its brother, its sister, its mate. She planned to pop the husband into her mouth and let his dying liquid hydrate her parched tongue while his wife looked on, her acidic screams silent in the sunny kitchen.

She was Cronus, huge and powerful, eating of his own fruit, one child at a time. Neither she nor the Titan ate out of hunger, but out of fear and desperation.

As she removed the seeds from each hemisphere, she noticed one had split, its crooked stalk of birth emerging from the rigid husk. The beige shell had given way to the insistent nudging of the delicate sprout inside.

Pessimistic, she planted the seed, sure that it would die like everything else she'd attempted to cultivate. No lush job, no fruitful marriage, no fertile womb — a barren existence soured further by loneliness.

The seedling paid no attention to her past failures. In its ignorance, it continued to thrive in the grey stone pot on the back porch. It wobbled and stretched; it reached upward and pulled itself toward the sky.

Hope broke through the dusty soil of her heart and she began to speak to the little tree. About the nasty email from her boss, the rude man at the train station who pushed past her to take the last available seat. Even told it about the property maintenance man who never missed an opportunity to make a cruel comment.

One evening as she arrived at her apartment, he saw her in the parking lot and jeered, his laugh braying and nasal. The plant shuddered with outrage, losing a few sweet-tart scented flowers in the process. Its empathy soothed her and she touched the tip of a leaf with her ring finger.

The next day, a blue-aproned boy at the garden center answered her question about the best fertilizer for citrus trees. "They love organic."

But she couldn't leave the store. A neglected grapevine had its long tendrils wrapped around her waist. She untangled herself and gave the vine a gentle pat as she listened to its inaudible plea.

As she lifted her purchase from the car, she cringed at a familiar laugh. He watched her struggle with the heavy pot until she got it on the back patio next to the young tree.

When his heavy footsteps landed on her stairs, she scurried inside and locked the door. She didn't bother to investigate his muffled screams until all of his struggling subsided. Long enough to uncork a bottle of red and let it breathe.

On the back patio in the spring afternoon sunshine, her lush plants bookended a dried-out husk. It crumbled to powder when she stepped over it to reach for the ruby red globe hanging from one of her baby's branches. Sangria would be nice.

Sounds in the Night

Ronna Magy

She rushes down the path to the lake, the feel of the stones familiar underfoot. A trace of black sandal strap dangling from her right ankle, a hint of gold from the unbuckled clasp takes her back to the bedroom where, earlier in the evening, she dressed for the dance. She'd pulled on the black dress, run a brush through her hair, and set the gold necklace, once her mother's, in place around her neck. She had so looked forward to seeing old friends.

Her bare feet race beyond the cobblestones onto green moss. Underfoot, she feels the place where the rough mat parts and opens up to bare earth. She senses the streak of blood and its shadow as they drip from her wound, feels the rip in her dress, torn from the neck. Her mother's necklace is gone.

She doesn't know if she is running now, or has been running, or is still running. It doesn't matter. The lake lies in front of her, somewhere beyond the trees. She hopes that from a nearby spot its dark pool will glisten up at her in the glow of the moon. In her arms she carries her baby, Adam, wrapped in the blue blanket knit by her aunt, finished just days before his birth.

She has to get away from him, the man she met the other day on her walk through the woods. She was looking through the bay laurel branches, up at the sky, as he approached. His beard, a slight gray stubble along the line of his chin. His eyes, a cloudy, overcast blue. He had the feel of somewhat familiar in his worn corduroy shirt, faded jeans, and cracked brown boots. Jackknife tucked neatly beneath his belt.

Cutting a green branch, he broke a leaf off for her to smell. *Not beautiful, but they sure smell good,* he'd said. The familiar smell of the leaves and his gesture put her at ease; brought to mind the smell of warm stew spiced with bay leaves as it simmered on the old porcelain stove.

The sparkle between trees... What was it? Not more of his knife, she fears, and through her head passes a swoon as she recalls the horror of the blade.

If only I can remain steady, find the shore, the water, and the boat, she tells herself. *If only I can get there... Before he gets to me... Before the blood runs out.*

What was that noise? A rustle of leaves? What was that? A small animal rushing along the stones? And that? The waves?

Now, she thinks she sees the outlines of the dock and the boat. The oars. The shadows of where the boat is tied to its moorings. The rope coiled in a rough pile along the dock. Perhaps she hears the waves as they lap against the hull. *If only I can get there before him,* she tells herself, *find my way down the path to the water and the dock.* Not far from where she stands, she hears waves lapping on shore. Nighttime waves as they come up onto the land. *Ssh,* she woos the baby. *Ssh,* she holds the infant lovingly to her breast. *Ssh,* she says, and pulls it in closer to her. *Mmm,* she hums to the child softly under her breath as she approaches the shore. *Mmm,* she speaks to the child almost silently in the ways of a mother.

The light of the moon shines through the trees, as the glint of a knife blade flashes above her in the moonlight.

Saving Celia

Mariana McDonald

The oak trees in the park were centuries old, their heavy branches thick with Spanish moss. As they grew over scores of years, the trees widened and stretched, taking on new shapes. From a distance the puffs of moss looked like lacey bits of fabric dangling unevenly from the branches' cuffs, as if nature knew no tailor.

The trunk of one tree was wide and full of scars, some from growth and some from human carving. A three-foot wide stretch mark ended on top in an inverted V, leaving the tree bare of bark in an inviting triangle that could be considered by those with imagination a kind of throne.

The woman walked past the sloping edge of the bayou and toward the trees, scrutinizing them, testing the firmness of the ground and wetness of the grass. Her thick dark hair was jumbled under a cap and a jacket hung open around her hips. She had flung her small backpack over one shoulder.

She saw the stark throne from the edge of her eye, and twirled back around to take it in. This is a good spot, she thought. Open and private at the same time. Not a lot to reckon with after, she reflected, as she slid her back into the triangle and bent her knees to sit down. She unzipped the pack and began to reach for its contents when she remembered, suddenly, Celia's tree, the one she'd given her that summer. Celia had fashioned a half-foot tall tree out of bits of silver wire and given it to her to say thank you. She would never say the words themselves, as that would be to admit what had happened.

It had been a New Orleans summer evening, humidity sticking to the skin like a swarm of flies. The only way to stand it was to move and keep on moving, power-walk away the heat by sculpting a breeze with one's motion. Her route was two-plus miles, tolerable evenings after work. Going down Green Street was off the path, but she hadn't seen Celia for a while, and the extra paces would do her good. She marched toward her friend's rented shotgun.

Walking in place, she knocked on the door. She glanced at Celia's battered sedan parked by the side of the house. Silence persisted.

Maybe she's taking a nap, she thought. But where are the boys? Wouldn't she have picked them up from day care by now? She pushed at the door, which creaked open, and entered the house, calling her friend's name. She stepped over evidence of a toddler and a pre-schooler: small plastic trucks, a diaper, a dirty tee-shirt, pop-up books.

She walked past empty bedrooms toward the bathroom when she felt a rush of bile that made her gag.

Celia was sprawled in the bathtub semi-conscious, and a half dozen empty pill bottles were strewn on the floor like Mardi Gras beads. Next to them on a page of bright white school-ruled paper was scrawled, *Dear babies, I'm sorry, I can't.*

She leapt into the tub and pulled Celia out by the arms. She looked at the labels of the empty bottles: Depakote, Xanax, Valium.

We've got to get you to the hospital, she screeched. She lifted her friend's limp body, sliding her across the hall to the living room floor.

Celia, where are your goddam keys? she wailed as she scurried about the living room, searching. She spotted them on the kitchen counter. She pocketed the keys and pulled Celia's arm around her shoulder as she lugged them both out the door to the car.

She pulled into the ER entrance and called out, *Help! She... took something!* A nurse came rushing to the car. Celia was maneuvered onto a gurney and whisked away.

What happened the next few hours would always be a blur. She could only remember the clerk quizzing her, asking questions about insurance and relatives that she couldn't answer, as she waited for word about Celia.

Finally a doctor walked quietly to where she was sitting in the waiting room.

She's going to be all right, the doctor announced. *But she'll need short-term supervision and long-term support.*

When Celia finally was wheeled out and stepped away from the wheelchair, standing on her own, pale and drawn, they both said nothing. In silence, they got into the car.

The boys are at their father's, Celia whispered in the car as they headed out of the parking lot. *Please just take me home.*

She took Celia home and stayed with her a while as she slept. In the days and months and years that followed, they never spoke of what had happened.

She'd kept the little metal tree for years, long after she'd lost touch with Celia and the boys.

A breeze touched her cheek. The oak tree's trunk remained still as she sensed the movement of the smallest, thinnest branches in the wind.

Oh shit, she said, thinking about her own long-past-toddlers. *Shit.*

She took the small revolver from the backpack. She unlatched the safety. She flipped the barrel and emptied the bullets into the palm of her hand.

She stood up and walked to the bayou, tossing the bullets like bread to the ducks.

Then with one great swing, she threw the revolver into the water, where it landed with a splash like a stone.

Spear Maiden to Persephone

Geri Lipschultz

All superheroes are violent, so do not marry one, but all who are not superheroes are also violent. A discovery made by one of the female explorers.

Empty pages: my life has been that for a while. I've stepped into someone else's book. I've skated on their pages. I've relinquished my religion and my height. I've given up my hair for a good cause. They must pulverize, snip off the tips of my daughter's fingers. This will make the bees sing again. Birds will flutter at our windows again. Cicadas will stop preparing for war.

Just a small sacrifice, and the snow falls on the buds of the magnolia, what is left after the great storm. The land has sued the sky for divorce. We walked on the side of the roads, trying not to look at the torn fences, trees fallen. A dry earth, the biologist said, that longs for its herds. We must eat the animals, round them up according to schedule. Tie them to a hook in the earth's core, where the elders lie.

Her fingertips have grown back. Even the whorls. Her little ridges. I lick them, watched by the cat, whose very tongue is a ridge. His eyes like those of owls. He curls around my daughter's fingers and stares.

How a daughter came to this world, I will tell you. I don't have the permit, so do not repeat what I say. I caught her, wrestled with a squirrel for her. He was atop the maple, chewing buds, and she was up there, as well, had climbed up to see the world. She didn't want to come down. I thought to send my cat, but he lives indoors. His purrs inflate the house. I didn't want to come home to a sinkhole, didn't want the house to lose its balance, to tip.

My fingers bleeding, my tongue full of blood. My eyes dry for the collection of tears that I gave to the Jehovah's Witnesses. Yes, you can have them, I said. You have lovely wool that was last seen on a drove of sheep. Dolly gave up her coat, and I gave up my tears.

It's a long story but must remain short. Otherwise, court-martial. Otherwise, prison. Otherwise, the degree stays in the file, and the file will be deleted. I will have to be observed. I will have to show my registration. A small box of index cards with the information written by hand. A relic of my twenty years of labor, for which I was paid a teaspoon of sugar. It adds up. My daughter will tell you. I will send her out into the world with all her whorls reborn, on a berth of roses, her rosette of gardenia, her garden of Eden, her evening posies. Wave goodbye and smile.

I buried a blade under her arm. It's a virgin knife, passed down, like the Bible we all carried down the aisle.

The Dead Letters

Diane Arrelle

She sat on the porch of the weathered beach house and watched the storm approach from the north, the growing clouds rapidly devouring the blue sky. The wind picked up as the green ocean turned pewter-gray and whitecaps danced across the surface. The first drops fell, wind-driven like a million tiny needles, and she jumped up and dashed inside, protecting the white envelopes she'd been holding.

Looking around the tiny cedar shake bungalow, she began to cry, her tears mixing with the rain she hadn't bothered to wipe off her face. She'd love it here. It was the first place she'd been able to call home since she ran away as a teen twenty years before.

She sat on the overstuffed couch as the thunder boomed a few miles away. She didn't have a lot of time, but she really wanted to sit and think for a few minutes. She remembered the first time she'd seen this house four years ago. It was picture-postcard perfect on a sunny spring day, the azaleas and daffodils were blooming, the old lady on the porch was knitting as a cat slept at her feet.

She waved and called, "Hi, lovely day," and was surprised by her boldness.

The old woman smiled. "Well, hello to you. Yep, it sure is lovely. Don't know you, do I? The memory's fading a bit and so is the eyesight. You the Borden's daughter?"

Continuing on down the beach would have been the normal thing to do, but she was compelled by some unknown force to stop and chat. The little voice, the cunning survivor, whispered in her head, "Say yes."

The young girl she'd once been shouted, "Tell the truth!"

"No, I'm not from around here. My name's, uh, my name's Danni," she said, surprised she'd used her real name.

"Well, I'm Eileen Albertson. Glad to meet you, Danni. Come on up and sit a spell. I have fresh iced tea and no one to talk to since my sister passed last year 'cept the mailman and the delivery boys."

Danni, finally Danni again after 15 years on the road, smiled and accepted.

Now, after four years, Danni knew she had to leave. Eileen's deceased sister, Elaine, was turning 100 years old and the family who ignored the aging sisters except for Christmas cards were coming next week to celebrate. Danni was sure they were coming to make sure they got in the will. After all, the two sisters had lived on a moderate trust that appeared in their bank account like clockwork once a month, along with their Social Security, and the beach house had to be worth a fortune, not to mention all the heirloom jewelry.

"Vultures!" Danni muttered then laughed through her tears. "What the hell, I'm no better, except that I loved Eileen."

She thought back to that fateful day when she was taken in by a ninety-one-year-old woman and treated like family for the first time in her life. After a few months together, Eileen woke Danni at sunrise and whispered, "I did something very bad last year, come on, I'll show you."

Bleary-eyed, Danni followed the aged woman out to the locked garage. Eileen opened the door, motioned Danni to follow, and pointed to a covered shape in the corner.

"Please, don't think badly of me. I didn't know what to do, I needed the money to live and pay the taxes on this place. Beach property is expensive, you know, and I may be old, but I'm not senile."

Danni tiptoed over to the shape, picked up the edge of the tarp, and looked underneath. With a shriek she dropped it like it bit her.

"Who is it?" she gasped.

"It's Elaine." Eileen answered calmly. "She died one afternoon, and as I went to call 911, I realized no one really sees us and the money is direct deposit so I decided to, uh, keep her alive a while longer so I could afford to stay here."

Danni looked under the tarp again, studying the dead woman. "Smart move."

"Thank you. Danni, I was sure you'd keep my secret. Now, I have a big favor to ask of you. When I die, keep me here as long as possible and live on the money. But when you have to leave, cremate Elaine and me and put us on the beach to blow as we will."

Eighteen months ago she had found Eileen dead in bed, and she's put the sisters together in the garage.

The thunder rumbled directly overhead. It was time to move. She walked to the shriveled sisters now seated in the living room, kissed them both on the forehead, and went into the kitchen. She lit several candles, turned on the gas stove pilot, then addressed one of the letters she'd been holding to the lawyer and on the other one, the letter from the relatives, she wrote DECEASED: RETURN TO SENDER.

She looked around one last time, wondering if it would be the lightning or the candles that would do it. Grabbing her backpack, heavy with her inheritance, Danni went out into the rain. She didn't wait around for the explosion; she mailed the letters and then took off down the beach.

Although the house would be gone, the sisters would always be there, blowing around the beach. In a few weeks, after the will was read, Danni would be back, too.

Voice Mail For the Living:
In the Dark Out There

Beverly C. Lucey

People keep telling me to change our outgoing message. Not people, exactly. Friends. Some people don't know they're calling just me when they're calling you. So, I could change it. But I can't figure out if that's what you would want me to do, just because you died. That's just one *more* thing we never discussed ahead of time.

Right now, when you just said you'd get back to me, I'm still believing it. So that feels good. For a second. Your voice is full of possibility. You'd get back to me because you'd want to get back to me. You wanted to get back to pretty much anyone who called, I guess. I wish I was like that.

Assuming that every call could be a good thing, and not like Dorothy Parker said, "What fresh hell is this?" if the phone rang. Of course, she didn't have call screening, answering machines, and could only decide whether to get up and answer the bell or not. Probably she didn't, maybe three quarters of the time. She drank.

I wish I could drink. Contradict all those warning labels on my prescription bottles. I just got a refill on the sleep meds. Remember when one of the docs asked me if I "wanted something?" Ha! I wanted everything, not just something. But not those. Not then. Not when you might need me in the middle of the night. I did start taking them after the funeral, though. Funny, I've never thought of taking a bunch of them. Maybe it's because I know, if I want to, I can call and you'll answer. Anything is better than nothing.

Sometimes it makes me feel safer — that you'll answer the phone when no one is there. You know. Stalkers. Perverts. Telemarketers. All the same thing, I guess. Which means I'll probably leave it on.

I'm embarrassing myself, and I'm alone in the car. Just driving through Northampton, heading home. I went to Walmart. I suppose *that's* embarrassing, and I never would have done it if you were around, but you're not. I might have been feeling irritated about that.

So, to make it up to you, I stopped off at Aurelia for chocolate croissants. That would cheer you up no matter what else was happening. On oxygen or not. Now, I'm eating for both of us. Which reminds me. I never thanked you for not bugging me about my weight. I just took it for granted. It was me inside, after all. That never changed.

Speaking of weight, your daughter's quite a bit lighter. Why I called in the first place...is that I'm coming from the hospital. A girl this time. That would make you smile more than a pastry. It would if you were here, but you're not. Damn you.

Even though you knew what you'd be missing? I figured you'd hang on until she at least had this baby. You promised her. She reminded me of that at least three times tonight, hair all stuck to her forehead like when she was two and had a fever dream. Our baby.

Now, I'll get in the house and see you all over the place, your office, your notes, your rolls of pennies. It's the kitchen that looks so weird. I don't know where all the platters came from. You'd think people would label the bottom or something. Empty platters.

I'm just turning into the driveway. Now what? Go in and see if there are any messages?

Lights Out: Zelda at Highland Hospital

Kathryn Kulpa

It's almost nine o'clock. Time for the night nurse to come and tuck me into bed, and I'll make a show of yawning, of being dull and slow as most of us are, as they want us all to be. A placid vessel on a tranquilized sea. If I'm quiet, and wait until she's nodded off over her nurse-romance novel, dreaming of the handsome doctor-lover never to come for her, the old goat, I can slip out, and walk in the night air, and smell the jacaranda blossoms that almost smell like home — like home and the wide back porch where we drank sloe gin on long summer nights, after my parents had gone to bed, and kept our voices hushed, or tried to. My laugh that you loved, and the little green notebook where you'd write down things I'd say.

Was I your muse? Did I amuse? My feet were never still; my toes still tapped out the rhythms of dirty jazz, all those barracks dances and the juke joints we'd stop at, later and drunker. Mama never minded how late I came home; she'd been a belle in her youth and liked to know that somewhere young men fought their sheets in uneasy dreams and called my name, as they'd once called hers. One night, on a dare, you sipped champagne from my pale-pearl silk slipper, and it always smelled faintly winy after that, a smell that reminded me of moonlight, and sin, and you.

But I'm barefoot now and slip lightly over the cold tile floors. If I'm caught out after hours one more time, they'll tie me to the bed at night, and I'll be like poor old Elsie, with her red-chafed wrists and rubber continence panties, howling through the long nights like the lunatic that she, of course, is, that we all, of course, are.

I never wanted to be saved. I never wanted to be safe. I still don't. I let them take my days. The nights are still mine. Only in these dangerous moments of solitude can I remember myself. "One of those fast, dangerous girls" — a murmur of talk, overheard at the nurses' station. And for a moment I let myself imagine they were talking about me.

This, now, is my life. I rise early in the morning, so they won't suspect. Lying in bed past eight, wishing to be alone, refusing to eat: all these things are suspect.

I lob tennis balls back and forth to a tired attendant. My head throbs from relentless sunshine. I force a smile and pray for rain.

I long to lie in the shaded grass, barefoot, a tall glass of sweet tea beside me and a book to read, all in a lazy afternoon. But sloth is a sign of...something. I sit in a straight-backed chair. I pretend to listen to a lecture on home economics and the virtues of Victory Gardening and dream of the French dancer, Emma Livry, turned into a torch by the footlights. Still she turned, layers of tulle, magnificent in flame, to finish her grand jeté.

She never regretted beauty.

Emma Livry. It took me two days to remember her name. I'm not allowed my dance books. Dancing is dangerous; it might "trigger an obsessive episode." I'm not allowed to practice at the barre. I wear supportive cotton stockings. Me!

I'm sure my knees must weep.

I write Emma's name in a matchbook, so I won't forget her again. Matches are contraband, of course. Writing is discouraged, except for therapeutic exercises. A sign of neurosis, grandiosity.

I can't be you, Scott, no matter how often I let you be me.

I slip past the tennis courts, past the neat rows of seedlings, ready to carry us the last mile to victory. Tomatoes and broad beans can well, our lecturer told us.

But I am not content with a vegetable love. I will not plant my feet and root. I will not rot. I will not die on the vine.

I am not your ego, not your twin, not the girl you could have been.

I am tinder. I am tulle.
I am spark. I will fly.

"Urubamba Market, Peru" by Barbara Purinton

The Contributors

Diane Arrelle sold more than one hundred fifty short stories and two books. When not writing, she is a senior citizen center director. She resides with her husband, her younger son and her cat on the edge of the Pine Barrens in Southern New Jersey (home of the Jersey Devil).

Janette Ayachi is an Edinburgh-based poet with degrees from Stirling and Edinburgh Universities. She has been widely published and was shortlisted for a Write Queer London and a Lancelot Andrewes Award. She is the author of *Pauses at Zebra Crossings*, *A Choir of Ghosts* and editor of *The Undertow Review*.

Barbara Baer: While living in northern California, she runs Floreant Press and publishes regional women's writing. Her fiction recently appeared in *Wreckage of Reason* vol. 1 & 2. She is a teacher, journalist, and self-taught horticulturalist.

MaryEllen Baizley is an educator, literacy specialist, baton coach and mother of four amazing young people. She lives in Maine.

Jesi Bender is a writer and artist living in Upstate New York. (www.jesibender.com)

Tantra Bensko teaches fiction writing online, living in Berkeley. She has over two hundred stories and poems in journals, two books, with two more slated, and four chapbooks. She puts out other people's work with LucidPlay Publishing. She has an MFA from Iowa. (http://lucidmembrane.weebly.com)

Tara Campbell (www.taracampbell.com) is a Washington, D.C.-based writer of crossover sci-fi. With a BA in English and an MA in German Language and Literature, she has a demonstrated aversion to money and power, despite living in a city obsessed with both.

Chella Courington: With a Literature PhD and a Poetry MFA, she teaches writing and literature at Santa Barbara City College. Her recent work appears in *Nano Fiction, The Collagist,* and *SmokeLong Quarterly.* In 2011 Courington published *Paper Covers Rock, Girls & Women,* and *Talking Did Not Come Easily to Diana.*

Jodi Sh. Doff is a New York based writer and photographer. Her work has appeared in *xoJane, Penthouse, Cosmopolitan, Bust Magazine, The Olive Tree Review, Bearing Life; Best American Erotica; The Bust Guide To A New Girl Order;* and *Hos, Hookers, Callgirls & Rentboys.* She received her MFA from Lesley University where she advises a graduate seminar in memoir.

Catherine Edmunds' published works from Circaidy Gregory Press include the poetry collection *wormwood, earth and honey* and the novels *Small Poisons* and *Serpentine.* Her latest work is the tangled love story, *Bacchus Wynd.* (www.freewebs.com/catherineedmunds)

Mary Finnegan's work has appeared in *Farrago's Wainscot, Serendipity, The Bad Version, Shadows of the Mind Anthology, Fiction Brigade, Writing That Risks, Red Bridge Press, Real Lies, Zharmae Press, Tortured Souls, Scarlett River Press* and *Advances in Parapsychological Research* (Saybrook).

Janet Garber: Armed with a graduate degree in English, she deserted Academia. She ran off to Mexico and France for several years of wide-eyed adventure before settling back again in NYC. Over the years, she has moonlighted as a freelance journalist, reviewer, poet, and author.

Theo Greenblatt teaches writing at the Naval Academy Preparatory School, a situation she finds both rewarding and surreal. She has had work published in *Aesthetica Magazine*, *South Loop Creative Nonfiction+Art*, *Vermont Literary Review*, and a forthcoming anthology of women's writing entitled *Shifts*.

Melanie Griffin writes from Columbia, SC. When she's not working in HR at her favorite public library, she writes short stories, runs, and watches *Doctor Who*. Her short stories have been published in *Alligator Juniper* and upcoming *New Dead Families*.

Mick Harris is a writer and educator living in the SF Bay Area. She has had work published in *Pink Litter*. She works in an office, watches a lot of Netflix, bitches about life, and blogs at www.positivelysocialsix.wordpress.com.

Jessica Lynne Henkle has a BA in English and Art History from Boston University and an MFA in Writing from Pacific University. She is a writer, editor, book reviewer, and blogger who lives in Portland, Oregon. You can visit her at jessicalynnehenkle.com.

Donna Hill is a published author with numerous novels to her credit. She completed her MFA at Goddard College and currently is an Adjunct Professor at Essex County College, The College of New Rochelle and Medgar Evers College. She lives in Brooklyn with her family.

Hall Jameson is a writer and photographer who lives in Helena, Montana. Her writing and artwork has recently appeared, or is forthcoming in, *Swamp Biscuits & Tea*, *42 Magazine*, and *Eric's Hysterics*. When she's not writing or taking photographs, Hall enjoys hiking, playing the piano, and cat wrangling.

J. Christine Johnson: Short-listed for the Santa Fe Writers Project 2011 Fiction Award, her stories have appeared in *Stories for Sendai*, *Granny Smith*, *River Poets Journal*, and *Cirque*. She recently left a career as a wine buyer in Seattle to work on her first novel in the rain shadow of the Quimper Peninsula.

Kathryn Kulpa graduated from Mills College and Brown University. She teaches creative writing at the University of Rhode Island and Frequency Writing Workshops. She received the Mid-List Press First Series Award for *Pleasant Drugs* and her work has appeared in *Cleaver, Foundling Review,* and *Literary Orphans.* She served as a fiction editor for *Pif* and is now editor of *Newport Review.*

Amanda Larson is a writer, freelance artist, and farmer on beautiful Whidbey Island where she lives with her family and menagerie of critters. She enjoys nothing more than exploring the world through fiction and particularly through the speculative genres. She loves writing stories of all lengths.

Geri Lipschultz has work forthcoming in Pearson's *Introduction to Literature* and in Spuyten Duyvil's *The Wreckage of Reason: An Anthology of Contemporary Xxperimental Prose by Women Writers.* She was awarded a CAPS grant from New York State for her fiction and won the fiction 2012 award from *So to Speak.*

Beverly C. Lucey's recent publications include: first prize for fiction at Estonian National Broadcasting, Spring 2013; short work of fiction published in the Canadian anthology *Friend. Follow. Text.,* October 2013; and short work of fiction published in the British anthology *Scraps,* 2013.

Lisa Lutwyche has an MFA in Creative Writing, a BFA in Art, and a BA in Art History. Poet, playwright, watercolorist, and actor, she has published in the US and the UK. An Adjunct at Cecil College in Maryland (English and Fine and Performing Arts), she has taught Creative Writing and Watercolor at community arts centers for over twenty years.

Melissa J. Lytton is a freelance writer and graphic designer, specializing in science fiction and alternative lifestyles. She earned her MFA in Creative Writing from Goddard College in 2013. In undergrad, she was The University of Kansas' first Science Fiction Scholar and won the Edgar Wolfe Award in Short Fiction.

Ronna Magy lives in Los Angeles near the ocean. Ronna's recent work has appeared in: *Trivia: Voices of Feminism, MuseWrite, Off the Rocks, Where Thy Dark Eye Glances, Southern Women's Review,* and *Lady Business: A Celebration of Lesbian Poetry.*

Mariana McDonald's work has appeared in many publications, including *Fables of the Eco-Future, Southern Women's Review; Sugar Mule, Anthology of Southern Poets: Georgia; From a Bend in the River: 100 New Orleans Poets; El Boletín Nacional,* and *Feast.* She became a fellow of the Hambidge Arts Center in 2012.

Coelynn McIninch is an artist and professional photographer working in Massachusetts. She identifies as a "magpie by nature, but a science geek at heart." Much of her artwork is inspired by the play between technology, perception and cognition. To learn more about her work, visit her website at: www.coelynn. com.

Tania Moore's stories have appeared in *Quiddity, Kestrel, The Other Journal, Sheepshead Review, The Westchester Review, Light Quarterly* and *Opium online.* She was a finalist for the 2012 *bosque* Fiction Prize. She earned her MFA from Columbia University, where she was the recipient of the C. Woolrich Fellowship for fiction. She teaches creative writing.

Wendy Nikel: When not busy writing about time travel, magical islands or space ships, she enjoys drinking coffee, playing video games with her husband, and building Lego race cars with her two sons. Links to her previously published short stories can be found at wendynikel.wordpress.com/short-stories.

Patricia Flaherty Pagan (Editor) is the founder and editor at Spider Road Press. She earned her MFA in Creative Writing from Goddard College. Her short fiction recently appeared in *Spry Literary Journal, Robocup Compendium 2013, The Pitkin Review* and *Calico Tiger.* Connect with her at www.patriciaflahertypagan. com.

Barbara Purinton is working on a memoir in the MFA program at Goddard College. She is an ordained minister who lives in North Hero, Vermont and still serves churches part-time while she pursues her writing. She loves to take photographs of her family and the amazing world around her.

Carmen Rinehart is an expatriate mother of two from southern Louisiana who has lived in Asia and South America for the past decade. Her career as a freelance non-fiction writer is successful; however, she is exploring her more creative side through short stories, poems and flash fiction.

Eden Royce is a native Charlestonian whose great-aunt practiced root magic. She wishes she'd listened more closely. Her stories have appeared in anthologies by Kerlak/Dark Oak Press, Sirens Call Publications, and Blood Bound Books. She lurks around online at edenroyce.com.

Mardra Sikora recently retired as company president of a printshop in Omaha, NE, in order to pursue publication of her written work. The irony is not lost. Success is coming slowly with flash fiction, essays, and high-profile blogs. Check it all out at mardrasikora.com or connect via Twitter @Mardrasikora.

Miranda Stone began writing fiction and poetry as a child. She figured she was onto something when a relative asked why all her stories were so sad. Employing a minimalist writing style, her work is strongly influenced by the setting and culture of the Appalachian Mountains. She lives in Virginia.

Rebecca Waddell enjoys writing everything from children's books to adult fiction. Rebecca has been published in the spring 2010 edition of *Yosemite Journal*, the Halloween 2011 edition of the *SLO City News*, and *if & when Literary Magazine*.

Melissa Webster holds an M.A. in writing from The Johns Hopkins Writing Program. She has worked as an editor, clerk, cleaner, waitress, factory packer and chicken farmer. She currently lives in Harare, Zimbabwe, with her husband and three children, and works as a writer.

Acknowledgements

The editor and publishing team wish to thank the following people: Eileen Brunetto, Lani Longshore, Jo-Anne Rosen, the Flaherty sisters, Donna Hill, Renee Maynes, Rachel Fischer and Heather MacGumerait for their firm belief in the fledgling project even when it teetered on the edge of un-being. The editor wishes to acknowledge the work of Robocup Press in beginning the submissions process. She sends a million thanks to the gifted designer Jo-Anne Rosen, patient, wonderful submissions editor Steve Pagan, helpful submissions assistant Kessika Johnson and skilled copy editor Pamela Mooman for helping to bring the anthology to life. She also appreciates web consultant David Baizley for his marketing assistance. In addition, she expresses sincere gratitude to all of the talented folks in the Goddard College community, The California Writers Club, Tri-Valley Branch and at Inklings Publishing. Finally, the editor wishes to thank the Flaherty, Pagan, Holland and Nugent families for their consistent support of the project.

Made in the USA
San Bernardino, CA
20 August 2015